John T. Griffith

Rev. Morgan John Rhys

John T. Griffith

Rev. Morgan John Rhys

ISBN/EAN: 9783337195564

Printed in Europe, USA, Canada, Australia, Japan

Cover: Foto ©Raphael Reischuk / pixelio.de

More available books at **www.hansebooks.com**

Rev. Morgan John Rhys

"The Welsh Baptist Hero of Civil and Religious Liberty

of the 18th Century."

—BY—

JOHN T. GRIFFITH

Pastor of the FIRST BAPTIST CHURCH OF LANSFORD, PA.

Lansford, Pa., March 9, 1899.

(Copyrighted by J. T Griffith)

o o o o o o o

LANSFORD, PA.,

LEADER JOB PRINT.

1899.

CONTENTS.

	PAGE.
PREFACE	3

CHAPTER I.
A SKETCH OF THE LIFE OF MORGAN JOHN RHYS ... 7

CHAPTER II.
MRS. ANN LOXLEY RHYS ... 18

CHAPTER III.
THE WELSH MAGAZINE OF MORGAN JOHN RHYS ... 20

CHAPTER IV.
THE SUBSTANCE OF HIS TWO LAST SERMONS IN WALES ... 26

CHAPTER V.
THE ALTAR OF PEACE ... 29

CHAPTER VI.
A SERMON BY THE CELEBRATED MORGAN JOHN RHYS ... 36

CHAPTER VII
APPEALS IN BEHALF OF LIBERTY ... 51

CHAPTER VIII.
AN ORATION ON LIBERTY ... 55

CHAPTER IX.
BEULAH SETTLEMENT AND CHURCH ... 59

CHAPTER X.—FAMILY RECORDS.
RHEES FAMILY ... 74
LOXLEY FAMILY ... 77
LOWRY FAMILY ... 80

CHAPTER XI.
MORGAN JOHN RHEES, JR., D. D., a son ... 81

CHAPTER XII.
WILLIAM JONES RHEES, a grandson ... 82

CHAPTER XIII.
AN APPENDIX. ... 85

PREFACE.

—o—

A Word to the Reader:—

A few years ago I received a note from the Rev. J. Spinther James, M. A., Llandudno, North Wales, author of "The Ancient Welsh Church," "The Welsh Baptists," &c , &c., requesting me to gather all I could of the history of Morgan John Rhys, and if possible to get a sample of his hand writing. This prompted me to do all that I could to meet the above request. I found that I had some of his history already in my possession in the "Literary Essays" of Rev. L. Edwards, D. D., of Bala, and also in "Seren Gomer," by Rev. Thomas Lewis, of New-port, Wales, and in the Minutes of the Indiana Baptist Association, by Mr. J. F. Barnes; but still I did not have what I wanted and needed. In September, 1898, I wrote a note of inquiry to Rev. Robert Lowry, D. D., Plainfield, New Jersey. He directed me to Mr. B. O. Loxley, of Philadelphia, and Wm J. Rhees, Esq , of the Smithsonian Institute, Washington, D. C. The latter is a grandson of Morgan J. Rhys, and it is to him that I am indebted for all the materials of his grandfather found in this book, and for the sample of his hand writing, and for the family records on the Rhees and Loxley side. The Lowry record was sent me by Dr. Robert Lowry. I do not profess to have exhausted the materials or the history of M. J. R., but I have simply gathered these few facts and materials as a tribute of respect to the memory of one who deserves to be perpetuated in history as the hero of liberty in the 18th century. Doubtless after this has appeared others will prepare a more elaborate and worthy history of this great and noble man. Rev. H. G. Weston, D. D., L. L. D., and Mr. Robert P. Bliss, of Crozer Theological Seminary, will please accept my thanks for the loan of the "Altar of Peace."

JOHN THOMAS GRIFFITH.

LANSFORD, PA., March 9, 1899.

THIS LITTLE MEMORIAL VOLUME

is

Dedicated to

WM. JONES RHEES, Esq,

A grandson of M. J. R.,

Washington, D. C.,

WITH THE

SINCERE CHRISTIAN LOVE

OF

THE AUTHOR.

Morgan John Rhys.

CHAPTER I.

Dr. Armitage said that Morgan John Rhys was "the Welsh Baptist "Hero of Religious Liberty " Dr. Lewis Edwards, of Bala, Wales, said that he was "a man who had consecrated his life to fight against oppression and tyranny, and that he excelled as a defender of civil and religious liberty," and the Rev J. Spinther James, M. A , says "that he was a man tor in advance of his age,* and that he was not properly known nor properly appreciated by the age in which he lived, nor the one that followed. He was one of the few Welsh who belonged to that class that started the ball of the reformation to roll in Europe. Inasmuch as that ball in its course struck the British government and shattered it, so that the American colonies became free forever, and inasmuch as it also struck the oppressive monarchy of France, so as to cause the great revolution there, so that the English government was so possessed with fear that the lives of all who advocated liberty were in danger," M. J. R. became one of the objects of its persecution, as we shall see. "It is in connection with the history of such men as M. J. R. that the progress of the world is to be studied." (See Seren Gomer for Sept., 1898, pp 257, 258)

Hence no apology is needed for calling the attention of all who love liberty to the history of the above noble character even though it may be brief.

Morgan John Rhys was a son of John and Elizabeth Rees, of Graddfa, Llanfabon, Glamorganshire, South Wales, where he was born Dec 8, 1760. Inasmuch as his father was a prosperous farmer, M. J. R. received the best educational advantages that were possible in that age. He united with the Baptist Church of Hengoed, where, also, he began to preach and whence he went to Bristol College in August, 1786. He only remained one year at Bristol, for on Nov. 17, 1787, he was ordained as pastor of the Penygarn Baptist Church, Pontypool. We have

---

*This is seen in the fact that he formed a society to translate and circulate the Scriptures freely at least twelve years before there was any thought of the British and Foreign Bible Society.—Spinther.

a report of him preaching at the Association at Llanerchymedd in 1788. In the minutes of the Association that was held at Hengoed in 1791, there is a note stating that the church at Penygarn complains that their pastor is about to leave;" but no reason for his leaving is given. The spirit of travelling was strong in M. J. R., and he did not confine his service to the Baptists. We have an account of him being at the Independent Chapel at Llanwrtyd in the year 1791. Rev. D. Williams Troedrhiwdalar, died in 1874, at the age of 95 years. He said that he heard him preach twice on Easter Monday, 1791, at Gelynos, Llanwrtyd. David Jones, formerly of Penygarn, was with him. A man named Morgan Waters was converted under the ministry of the strangers. He became a useful member at Gelynos for 40 years, and his desire was to be buried in the Chapel at the spot where he sat when he heard the ministry that was the means of converting him to the Lord. Rev D. Williams was one of the subscribers of the magazine of M. J. Rhys. (See Dr. Phillips in Seren Cymru, May 17, 1867.)

M. J Rhys was at the Association at Swansea in 1791, and at the Association at Hengoed on the first Wednesday and Thursday of June of the same year. He went to France soon after this.* He believed that the Revolution had opened the way for the circulation of the Bible and the gospel in that country.

One who resided in France at that time wrote as follows: "There is religious liberty here for all without distinction, and every sect can preach in the churches without opposition from any. The Bible has already been translated into the language."

(Dr. Rippon's Baptist Register, 1798, p 465) Perhaps that M. J. R. had heard of this, and such news was sufficient to stir him, inasmuch as he was full of zeal, and ready to improve all the blessings of Liberty. After having been in France a few months, he returned to Wales (having been hindered by the war) and settled in Carmarthen town, where he started a book store and a printing press He was at the Association at Moleston in 1792, and was the Moderator. He preached at that Association, Welsh and English in the same sermon. In the minutes of this Association we find the following resolution: "At the request of Brother M. Rhys, it was agreed to request the churches to raise a collection towards sending the Word of the Lord to the French, and to send

*The following paragraph appeared recently in a newspaper in France, viz, Echo, de, la Verite:—"In the year 1792 Mr. Rhys, a gospel minister of Pontypool, Wales, came to Paris to explain the Word of God. He believed that the time had come, and he hoped that the people had become tired of the oppression of kings and Romish priests, and that they were ready to take advantage of the freedom that he proclaimed. Mr. Rhys rented a hall in which to preach the gospel, and to distribute Bibles to the people. But things turned out contrary to his thoughts, hence he left."
—Rev. Thomas Lewis.

it to Mr. Williams, of Cardigan, that he may send the money to those who were to distribute the Bibles that came out in the language of that country." About this time he persuaded his friend, Joshua Watkins, of Llanwenarth, to come to him. He also was a popular preacher, but had not yet been ordained. These two young men (M. J. Rhys, 31 years old, and Joshua Watkins, 22 years old) worked together in the book business and the printing. Prior to this and after this M. J. R. labored to establish Sunday Schools through the country, and at the Association that was held at Cwmdu in 1793 a resolution was passed "to advise the churches to make an effort to have Welsh schools to teach the youth to read the Scriptures. In the year 1793, four numbers, 6d each, of his magazine were issued, and one in February, 1794

In his work in establishing schools, Sunday and week evenings, he published a book for that purpose, entitled, "A Guide and Encouragement to Establish Sunday Schools and Weekly, in the Welsh Language through Wales, with lessons easy to learn, and principles easy for children to understand, and others who are illiteral." "Train up a child in the way he should go, and when he is old he will not depart from it."— Solomon, Carmarthen. Printed and for sale by J. Ross, August Street For sale also by J. Daniel, Market street; T. Evans, Machynlleth, and by ministers of the Gospel and others who wish the success of the cause through Wales 1793. Following this first page we have a "Preface" in two pages—then "the order of the Sunday Schools, the mode of conducting them, instructions to teachers as to the way to read correctly. Then we have the alphabet and lessons in spelling, that cover 24 pages. Then we have portions of Dr Watt's Catheehism, and some of his hymns for children, and a few prayers for them, and instructions respecting punctuation in reading, arithmetic, the way to count time, &c. The book is well printed and contains 48 pages; the last thing in the book is a "Letter to the Welsh from the Agents of the Welsh Magazine " In his preface to this book M. J. Rhys says that he had had an opportunity to have a talk with Mr. Raikes, of Gloucester, respecting the Sunday Schools. (A copy of this book is now in the possession of Rev. T. Lewis, Baptist Minister, Newport, Mon., Wales.) Who can estimate the amount of good accomplished through this little book in Wales?

Dr Jenkins, of Hengoed, says that M. J Rhys came to the place where he lived in 1793—"An highly esteemed minister named Morgan Rhys came this way; * * * He labored diligently * * * to agitate the idea of establishing Sunday Schools in Wales, before they had begun with any other religious denomination in the principality. He came through Llangynidr as well as other places to preach, and to urge the people to establish Sunday Schools and week evening; and he had written a small book worth 3d for beginners. I bought one of them.

By having that book, and a few lessons for a short time in a night school that was kept from house to house in the neighborhood, with a little help from my master at home, I had the invaluable privilege of learning to read the Word of God." (Autobiography p. 13)

The above Mr. Jenkins was a farmer's servant at Llangynidr at the time he bought that little book from Mr. Rhys, but he became the distinguished Dr. John Jenkins, of Hengoed, of which he was pastor for fifty years or more, and which was also the mother church of Mr. Rhys himself. It is claimed that Mr. Rhys established a Sunday School at Hengoed before he went to Bristol, i. e , before August, 1786, for he did not reside at his old home after that. In a letter that Mr. Raikes wrote on July 27, 1787, to Mr. W. Fox, he says: "I have sent you my paper this week, that you may see that we are extending towards Wales." (See Robert Raike's biography, p 107.)

Rev. Mr. Lewis, of Newport, Wales, from whose article on M. J. R. I have had all the facts thus far in this sketch, says that being very anxious to know how much the Gloucester Journal contained respecting Wales, he wrote to Mr. Chance, the editor, who very kindly answered as follows, without delay: "There is a letter briefly noticing the celebration of the anniversary of Sunday Schools at Cardiff. No names or more precise information appears." What a pity that the names of the participants were not given! An anniversary is held at the close of the year, hence there must have been Sunday Schools at Cardiff and the surrounding country in 1786, and perhaps before that. Mr. Lewis thinks that the school of M. J. Rhys is found in this period. One special characteristic of M. J. R. was quickness with all things. After having thought of some good plan, he would put it into practice at once. He had known of the schools of Mr. Raikes since the year 1780, or soon after that, and he could not remain long without attempting the same thing. The schools that had been begun by Mr. Raikes had increased by 1786 to 250,000 pupils. That was wonderful progress in five years (Gregory p. 90.) Mr. Raikes says in 1786 that the "dissenters" of all denominations worked with all their might with the Sunday School. One of the chief ones in this work was Mr. Fox. He was a native of Gloucester, but at that time he was a deacon in the Baptist Church of Prescott St., London

M. J. Rhys preached at the Association which was held at Ebenezer Anglesey in 1794, when "the churches were exhorted to continue to establish Sunday Schools to teach the youth and others to read Welsh." July 2nd, after the Association, M. J. Rhys preached at Glynceiriog, when John Edward and Thomas Jones were set apart But although he was thus in the midst of his popularity and usefulness, yet the time had come when he must leave his native land and flee to America

which he did August 1st, 1794, which was less than a month after he
had preached at Glynceiriog. The manner in which he left Wales and
the reason why he left is graphically described by the Rev. T. Lewis in
the article already referred to, and for the sake of the English reader I
will translate it verbatim: "I frequently made inquiries in Carmarthen
(Mr. Lewis was a pastor of a Baptist Church in Carmarthen for several
years.—G.) whether he had been imprisoned; I searched the records of
conviction; I questioned the Jailor and Mr George Thomas, the Town
Clerk; but I failed to find any evidence that he had ever been punished
or arrested, yet it is easily to believe that he was constantly in danger,
for we find the following words in his Reasons for Going to America.—
"We are not without seeing this persecuting spirit already. Many of
our fellow-countrymen say that hanging or burning is too good for us;
that we should be tortured and torn in pieces by wild animals But
what for? For nothing in the world but for desiring their welfare, and
for trying to open their eyes to see their civil and religious rights, but
thus far they love darkness rather than light." (p. 11.) To show the
danger to which M. J. R. was exposed we might note that Rev Thomas
Evans (Thomas Glyn Cothi), a Unitarian minister, who was a very
zealous advocate of civil and religious liberty, was imprisoned in 1776 at
Carmarthen for two years, and he was twice in the pillory. He was
imprisoned for defending liberty—this was the only charge that could
be brought against him.* (See his history in Gardd Aberdare, pp 89-110

The reader will see that M. J Rhys left very suddenly for America.
Shortly before this he intended to publish a hymn book and for that

---

purpose he was soliciting subscribers from the churches. Whilst in the midst of his plans he fled. How are we to account for this? I received the following explanation of this difficult matter from Mr. E. Alguin Evans, one who had been a school master all his life time in the town of Carmarthen. He would have been over a hundred years old had he been alive now (in 1891). The facts were frequently repeated to him by the Rev. Joshua Watkins, pastor of Prior Street Church, who died in 1841, aged 72 years. It happened thus: "In the year 1794 a Mr. Reed kept a hotel on the grounds where the Town Hall now stands. Morgan Rhys and his friends used to meet in a private room at this hotel. One night, about the close of July in the year stated, a stranger came suddenly in and asked for lodging there. After having had it, and been seated, he asked Mr. Reed if he knew a person in town by the name of Morgan Rhys. He received an affirmative answer, with the additional remark that Mr Rhys was a very good and a very respectable man. Then the stranger gave a hint that he had been sent from London, and that he had a warrant to arrest Morgan Rhys and to take him to the Capital (London). Mr. Reed promised to take the bailiff to the house of Mr. Rhys the next morning. Mr Rhys happened to be in the hotel at that time, but in another room. Mr. Reed went to him and told him all, and also told him to flee at once without any delay.

After Mr. Rhys had sent word to his friend, Mr. Watkins, and had given him some instructions, he fled, walking to Lampeter, and from thence to Newtown where he took a conveyance for Liverpool. After he had reached that place he made arrangements to sail for America, August 1st, but before he sailed Mr. Watkins reached Liverpool with clothes, etc., for Mr. R. They parted very sorrowfully, and by parting Mr. R. gave instructions and counsels to his friend as to the best course for him to pursue in his trials. They parted forever on the earth. Such is the account that Mr. Lewis gives of the manner and occasion of leaving Wales for America. He wrote a diary of his voyage, and as there are a few extracts in the article referred to they will be interesting to the English reader.

August 1st, 1794, under sails about half past two in the Port Mary, Capt. Kennedy. Delightful wind with some rain until we came to the main sea. So may the spirit of myself and my friends be whether the weather be unseemly or pleasant.

August 2d. I rested pretty well considering my new situation among so many different kinds of people—Welsh, English, Scotch, Germans and French, and all in a small portion of the vessel. Among them there are two physicians, one priest, two preachers and several kinds of tradesmen. I think that there is a better place here to gather general information than to learn special morals from many of them. However, the wind turns and all the people—men, women and children begin to sicken, the sea swells and throws up its waves and cares no more for the pomp of men than if they were flies. Yes, so fearfully is its aspects that the strongest of men tremble before its majesty and roughness. Ah, me! The women begin to howl, and the dishes begin to roll, and the children begin to cry, and the men begin to waver, and my bowels begin to fight with all the food that is needful to support nature. But Oh! my spirit, trouble not thyself, the body shall be renewed and the storm shall cease; be not afraid, God holds the sea in the palm of his hand and the winds in his fist. The night is nearing, and all the friends are in trouble. We had a little rest.

August 3d. The morning of the first day of the week. The wind continues contrary and quite strong. I did not rise out of my hammock all day. Oh! my soul, when didst thou spend a Sabbath like this before? Brother J. Davis is pretty well, and takes care of his children, and sings:

> "Bydd melus glanio draw—
> Nol bod o don i don,
> Ni gawn roi ffarwel maes o law
> I'r ddaear hon."

The literal meaning of the above is:

> "Sweet it will be to land beyond—
> After having been from wave to wave,
> We soon shall say farewell
> To this earth."

Whilst he was singing these words I changed them thus:

> "We soon shall say farewell
> To this storm."

August 4th. The second day of the week—a little better and the wind more calm. The most of the friends came to eat and came up on deck. I have begun to read and henceforth I hope to be able to read and write more minutely. The wind is still in the West, and we are not able to make much progress—something like the children of Israel in the wilderness which was rough in its course. So are we on the ocean by trying to sail against the wind. We must travel much before we can make scarcely any progress. But at last there is some hope that we shall come into port with song.

August 5th. The meditations of the night troubled me as I thought of my weaknesses and frequent lapses that the world knows nothing of. But in the midst of the mixture I had the testimony that God in Christ was my only safe refuge. I renewed my covenant and vows if I shall have strength to serve my Lord and my fellow creatures, and to act faithfully towards all men. I rose before all the family to read and study, which I intend to do throughout the voyage, if I shall have moderate health. This day dawned so calm that we could scarcely know whether the sea moved. Too much calmness is almost as obstructive to the voyage as too much storm. Too much ease in religion is often more injurious than many temptations. "Count it all joy when ye fall into divers temptations." Though the chastisement for the present time is not pleasant, yet it drives the soul to the throne of grace and worketh an eternal weight of glory. In the evening a little rain fell, and generally when rain comes we get a breeze also. When the soul is full of sap the entire person sails to Immanuel's land.

August 6th. We are yet within sight of Wales and the Isle of Man. With all my love to my native land, yet it is full time for me to lose sight of it. So each one who travels towards eternal happiness desires to lose sight of the vanity of this world. * * * In the evening we saw a large number of herring; they are consumed by the large fish as the common people are destroyed by some of the gentlemen. There are tyrants in the sea as well as on land with this difference—that all the inhabitants of the watery world will live either free or dead until they are conquered and their lives taken as a prey. I feel rather weak, I must go to bed.

August 7th. In the morning—the wind rather strong. At last the land of Wales is out of sight, and Scotland and Ireland appear in its place. The wind is rather against us—we must have patience. Be it so, though we have no reason yet to complain; yea, let it come as it may. I hope that I shall not be left to complain, but to bear all joyfully that I may meet with in this frail life.

August 8th. Sailing between Ireland and Wales. Oh! how beautiful the vessels appear when the wind fills their sails! Oh! my soul, may all thy powers be stirred; may they like sails receive the Heavenly breezes and sail towards the desirable haven! I feel some sorrow in my spirit for the need of an opportunity to hold public worship. Though true religion is personal and eternal, yet the fellowship of the saints and the right use of all the ordinances of God's house tend to increase the grace and knowledge of the believer.

August 9th. We are again on the borders of Wales. Behold Holy Head and the rocks of Carnarvonshire and the Island of Bardsey! Soon Cardiganshire and Pembrokeshire will come. Oh! my friends in Wales, my spirit is with you. * * * Some ought to remember the service rendered by the dissenters in this kingdom, but Israel is increasing notwithstanding all their oppression; and if so, let some look at it!

August 10th. Once again we have lost sight of the land of Wales.

Back of us St. David's could be seen in the morning. We are now sailing towards the Atlantic.

August 11th. Considering the season of the year the weather has been very cold, and the cold that I have had has made my body and spirit rather weak; yet I stand to read more than I remember.

August 13th. Though the wind is with us, yet we go on very slowly. We sail about from three to ten miles an hour.

August 15th. The sea to-day is like a boiling pot. I see majesty in its appearance; it sets forth the excellency of its Creator. * * * Oh! my soul, bless the Lord, whose way is in the sea and whose paths are in deep waters. Let that suffice from his diary.* At last he landed in New York about October 12th, 1794. In a sketch which was written by Dr. Nicholas Murray, his son-in-law, it is said that he was most kindly received by the Rev. Dr. Rodgers, then the pastor of the First Baptist church of Philadeiphia, and Provost of the University of Pennsylvania. Between these two there existed ever after a cordial friendship. Finding Civil Institutions of the country all in harmony with his political views, and nothing in the way of religious intolerance to fan his excitable feelings, the religious sentiment soon rose to the supremacy in his heart; and as if he had never turned aside from the ministry he again preached the gospel with great power and success. He was followed by admiring crowds wherever he spoke, and preached Christ with an earnestness and an unction, but rarely witnessed since the days of Whitfield.

He traveled extensively through the Southern States‡ and Northwestern Territory, preaching the Gospel of the Kingdom, and in search for a suitable location for a colony On his return to Philadelphia he married the daughter of Col. Benjamin Loxley of that city, who was an officer of the Army of the Revolution, and a man of high character and standing. After two years' residence in Philadelphia he, in connection with Dr. Benjamin Rush, purchased a large tract of land in Pennsylvania, which, in honor of his native country, he called Cambria. He also located and planned the capital of the county, to which he gave the name of Beulah. To this place he removed his own family, with a company of Welsh emigrants in 1798, which was increased from year to year by others from the principality. Here he was intensely occupied "with the duties which

---

*The above diary was in the possession of Mrs. Murray, a daughter of Morgan John Rhys. The Rev. Dr. Phillips, of Hereford, the agent of the British Bible Society, called to see her in Philadelphia, I think, some time after 1860, and when he saw the above diary in the handwriting of her distinguished father in Welsh, he borrowed it and took it with him to Wales, and extracts of it were published in Seren Cymru, (Star of Wales) of May 17th and 24th, and July 12th, 1867.

‡ See Appendix.

devolved upon him as a land proprietor, and as pastor of the Church in Beulah." (See Seren Gomer, January, 1899).

He again removed from Beulah to Somerset, the County Seat of Somerset County. One writer says that "about this time Thomas Mifflin, Governor of Pennsylvania, appointed M. J R. 'a Justice of the Peace for Quemahoning Township, Somerset County.' " Shortly afterwards the same Governor appointed him "an Associate Judge in and for Somerset County during good behavior" This commission is dated February 8, 1799. He held this office until January, 1800, when Thomas McKean, having succeeded Thomas Mifflin in the office of Governor of Pennsylvania, in about one month after being inaugurated appointed Morgan J. Rhys to the more lucrative situation of Prothonotary, Clerk of the Quarter Sessions, Oyer and Terminer, and Orphans' Court of Wills and Recorder of Deeds for Somerset County." This commission is dated as above, viz., January 29, 1800, and reads "until commission is superceded or annulled." (See Minutes of the Indiana Baptist Association, Pa , for 1889).

Yet in the midst of this honor and usefulness, when in the prime of his manhood, "he died of a sudden attack of pleurisy, and in the triumphs of faith, December 7, 1804. in the 44th year of his age. Indeed his departure seemed rather a translation than a death. "On the day of his death it seemed as if the heavens had been opened and he had been permitted to catch a glimpse within the vail 'The music, my love,' he said, 'it is so sweet ; do you not hear it ? When his wife said 'I do not,' he remarked: 'Oh, listen—now—now—'the angels sing come waft on high, we wait to bear thy spirit to the sky.' " He left a widow and five children to mourn his loss. His monument is seen in the cemetery of the First Baptist Church, Philadelphia. The following is a copy of what it says concerning him :—

A TRIBUTE OF AFFECTION

in Memory of

THE REV. MORGAN JOHN RHYS,

a Native of

Glamorganshire, South Wales,

Born December 8th, 1760,

Who Died at Somerset, Pennsylvania,

December 7th, 1804.

The Patriot desisted from the service of his adopted country,

The Christian ceased in this tabernacle to groan,

The Preacher of Jesus finished his testimony.

In 1806 his remains were removed to this family vault, from whence the Gospel of Jesus insures a resurrection.

> "Come waft on high, the heavenly envoys cry,
>   We wait to bear thy spirit to the sky.
> We heard with transport, bade the world adieu—
>   On their bright pinions up to heaven he flew,
> Now in the bosom of his Savior God
>   He finds a calm, a joyful, safe abode;
> His precious dust, here mingling with the ground
>   Rest hopeful till the Archangel's trumpet sounds,
> Then fashioned like its Lord, the soul shall see
>   The mortal put on immortality.
> Adieu, loved friend, soon shall our spirits meet
>   And cast their radiant crown at Jesus' feet."

(For the above tribute see "The Literary Essays" of Dr. Lewis Edwards, Bala, Wales, p 585.)

P. S.—The most of the above sketch has been translated from an article of Rev. Thomas Lewis, Newport, Mon., Wales, which appeared in Seren Gomer of April, 1891.

Mrs. Ann Loxley Rhees.

CHAPTER II.

Mrs. Rhees, the wife of Morgan John Rhees, was a daughter of Col. Benjamin Loxley, of Philadelphia, and Catherine Cox, of Freehold, New Jersey. She was born in Philadelphia, June 18th, 1775. Her father was Captain of the First Artillery Company of Philadelphia, in the Revolution. (For a brief sketch of his life, see chapter on Mr. William J. Rhees).

She became a member of the First Baptist church at the early age of 19 years and was baptized by the Rev. Stephen Ustick, who was then the pastor of the church. She was united in marriage to the Rev. Morgan John Rhees at Philadelphia, February 22d, 1796. In 1798 she removed with her beloved husband to Beulah, and from thence to Somerset, expecting doubtless to spend many years together, but this was not to be, for after having lived together less than nine years. the Lord took him to Himself, leaving her a widow with five children in the prime of her womanhood. But He Who had promised to be a husband to the widow, and a father to the orphan was still with her.

Mrs. Rhees was a woman of high character. On her great bereavement she returned to her native home where upon a limited patrimonial inheritance she educated her five orphan children. and lived to see them all not only members of the church of Christ, but filling posts of high honor and usefulness. Every one of her twenty grand-children, who lived to maturity, also became members of the church. She died in the Lord, April 11th, 1849, in the 74th year of her age.

Her memory is truly blessed. In an obituary of her it is said: "Endowed with a mind of the strongest original texture and polished by education and stored by reading and reflection, and by grace subdued to the most humble obedience to the truth. She was efficient in action, wise in counsel. strong of faith, and untiring in doing a spirit of self-sacrifice, connected with the deepest humility were her leading characteristics. There are but few, perhaps not one of the charitable institutions of her church or of its domestic or foreign missionary fields which do not contain in some way or form some record of her charity which never wearied in well-doing. But few have lived a life more consistent or lovely; but few have died a death more calm and confiding."

The following letter was addressed by Dr. Rush to' Mrs. Rhees in reference to the death of her husband, and it shows the writer's exquisite sensibility and sympathy as well as the high appreciation of Mr. Rhees' character:

"My Dear Madam—Accept of my sympathy in your affliction. While you deplore the loss of an excellent husband, I lament the loss of a sincere and worthy friend. His memory will always be dear to me. Be assured of my regard for you and your little family. May a kind and gracious Providence support you, and may you yet have reason to praise the orphans' father and the widow's God in the land of the living."

From my dear Madam,
Your sincere friend,
BENJAMIN RUSH.

Philadelphia, September 26th, 1805.

See Dr. William Sprague's Annals of the American Pulpit, Vol. VI, New York, 1860—quoted in part by Rev. T. Shankland Wales, in Seren Gomer, January, 1890.

The Welsh Magazine of Morgan John Rhys.

CHAPTER III.

In our sketch of the life of M. J. R., we referred to the five is-
sues of his magazine which he published in 1793 and 1794. The first
number was published in February, 1793. The first two numbers
were printed at Trefecca, which is an important place in the history
of Welsh Nonconformity. The Welsh Presbyterians have a college
here for the training of ministers. The third number was printed at
Machynlleth, which is situated near the mouth of the Dyfi, on the
boarders of Montgomeryshire and Merioneth. Indeed we find this
number was printed at two places. The name Machynlleth is on the
title page, on the back of which is printed these words: "We are
sorry to have to complain that this number, taking the work into consideration, is not all as well as we would wish". The reason is this:
It was printed at two different places, whether it was printed at
Machynlleth and Trefecca, or at Machynlleth and Carmarthen, where
the last two numbers were printed we cannot tell. Is it possible that
it was printed at Machynlleth, and some fourth place? If so, and it is
quite possible, we have five numbers printed at four different places.
What would the publishers of this age think of having to change
their printers and places every month? Morgan John Rhys had to do
this. May his name be ever dear to his countrymen, and may
his courage be theirs. It is not known who printed for him at Trefecca, but Ross & Daniels were his printers at Carmarthen, and one
Titus Evans, a native of South Wales, at Machynlleth. The subjects
treated of in the magazine vary from an essay on "Nothing," to one on
the "Omnipresence of God." Such subjects as these are treated:
"History of Tithes," "History of Religion in North America," "The
Duty of Keeping the Sabbath Day," "The Testimony of Josephus
Concerning Jesus," "The Value of Liberty," "Notes on the American
Indians," by Dr. Franklin, and the "Execution of the Queen of
France." We get some of the poems and letters of "Goronwy Owain,"
who died in America. Dafydd Ddu is represented by some excellent
poems, and we find two or three English poems, one of them which is
"A Poem of Gratulation on the Marriage of George the Third," writ-

ten by a Welshman of the name of Edward Edwards, of All Souls' College. The one object of the magazine was Liberty. It aimed at severing the connection between "Church and State." In this respect its aim was higher than that of the Welsh reformers. What was paramount with them was the reformation of the State Church, and some of them remained in it until they were liberated by death. The fact that they created a denomination without aiming at that is a proof of their ability and courage. This state of things was a source of trouble to Morgan John Rhys. He could not tolerate a State Church, but some influential men amongst those who had left it could do so. What they could not do was to tolerate an inactive and immoral church. In proof of this we may state that the Welsh Presbyterians as late as 1834 passed a resolution condemning the efforts of those who where aiming at disestablishment. The resolution was proposed at Bala, and that by the Rev. John Elias. It is only fair, however, to state that this denomination has done its share for disestablishment after this. Taking this fact into consideration as well as the fact that printing was so expensive and that it was so difficult to distribute a magazine throughout the principality, we do not wonder that only five numbers came out. But the work was not in vain. It may be rather difficult to point out details to prove this, but to raise such a clear strong voice as this in those superstitious and cowardly times was in itself a triumph. True words live longer than kind words very often. No, John Rhys was not a failure no more than John the Baptist. He had a mission, he delivered it, he escaped prison, and execution, and died in a free country. His example stimulates young Wales at the present time. What he fought for is close at hand, and he will become more popular than he has been. This magazine was worth its weight in gold, but was sold for six pence a copy. *We will now make a few extracts from this magazine.

---

*See "Essays in Welsh Literature," by Rev. I. D. Williams.

The History of Religion as to its Deterioration.

The first preachers of the gospel foresaw its deterioration. "Now the spirit speaketh expressly that in the latter times some shall depart from the faith, giving heed to seducing spirits and doctrines of devils" (1 Timothy IV 1). "That the man of sin shall be revealed the son of perdition" (2 Thes. II 3). Paul describes the apostacy of the church as though he could see it before his eyes, and it was not long before anti-Christ appeared to others in its cunning and oppressive spirit. When the mixing of vain philosophy with the simple doctrines of the gospel dissentions and disputes respecting all the doctrines of religion were begun in a cunning and cruel manner, and their purpose in each contention was to overthrow each other, new materials, like bones of contention, were constantly raised, and inconsistent expositions adopted and defended in an obstinate spirit. Each contention would cause some different conclusion, and every conclusion would produce some new objection and kindle a more cruel dispute—and all for supremacy. Who would establish the faith of Christians? By trying to trace things that were above the reach of man, and by setting questions that are too simple for us to notice them, new confessions were constantly increasing, and new distinctive words were coined and consecrated. The heads of doctrines and articles unreasonably multiplying, and in order to support their false doctrines, all the inconsistencies and scholarly false reasonings were used, and divine authority was ascribed more and more to the writings of men. As the doctrines of the gospel were forced from their primitive simplicity, they became unfit to touch the heart and to effect the conduct. Instead of being an incentive to holiness, they opened the way to all kinds of defilements and misery. The commandments of the gospel also, which as to their clearness and simplicity, bear with them authority, were obscured in such a manner as to confuse the mind rather than to arouse the conscience. Briefly, the rules of the gospel were gradually laid aside, and indulgence, penance, pardons, celibacy, pilgrimages to Rome, sheltering in monasteries, and a hundred other things too numerous to mention were appointed instead of the law of Christ. Also the Christian worship did not escape from the plague. It was soon disfigured with Jewish ceremonies and Pagan rites and others which the church constantly appointed at her pleasure. Baptism and the Lord's Supper were administered with such display and vain-pomp, that it was supposed that they were some awful mysteries. New virtues were ascribed to them and great authority used in consecrating them. The corruption of the latter ended in the monster transubstantiation, and in relation to the first it is scarcely credible to many how much unreasonable virtue is ascribed to it. It, they said, made men children of God, regenerated them and washed away their sins, and whoever died without it (as the teachers said in those dark times) would certainly be lost. Alas! How much folly came into the world with superstition? It is fearful to think that any are so foolish as to suppose that 'there is virtue in ordinances to take men to Heaven whether they be old or young. It would be too long to name all the rites that were gradually brought in. From glorying in the cross of Christ, they went to make use of the sign of the cross as a charm on almost every occasion; from praying for the dead they went to pray to the dead; from recalling to mind the martyrs, they went to worship them; from honoring their relics, they imputed to them the power to work miracles; from permitting pictures and images in their churches, they bowed down to them; fasts, holidays and feasts without number were constantly appointed by them, and short and simple prayers were extended to such a long and mixed form as to poison the worship with their insipious traditions. Not less dreadful was the corruption of the true spirit of Christianity. Though the Apostles were under Divine inspiration, they did not rule the faith of any (2 Cor , 1 24), but they bore with the infirmities of the weak in those things that were not hurtful to the essence of their religion (Rrom. XV, 1), &c., and their anathemas they kept for evil things. But, alas ! how soon their followers forgot the words of Christ? "The Kings of the Gentiles exercise lordship over them ; let it not be so among you" (Luke 22, 25, 26, Welsh version). But the Christians of the following ages changed the text thus: "Let it be so among you;" at least thus it was ; their creed and uncertain opinions and far-fetched inferences from the Scriptures, and all the sacred words which they had coined to set forth their view, must be received ; otherwise they would excommunicate a man to a place worse than purgatory ; and all this for a difference in words, when they would suffer all kinds of immorality, without even a threat of the lightest punishment. The work of the leaders of the church, as soon as the Emperors put the power in their hands, was to grasp for wealth, honor and the authority of citizenship. Also, priestly orders were greatly multiplied, bishops aspiring high: archbishops and patriarchs exalting themselves above them ; they not only grasped for every bishopric by the most unbecoming presumption, but every scheme was used to purchase it, one bishopric contending for supremacy in order to have control of men's consciences. This evil increased in all the churches so that they knew not for a long time where to establish the infallible chair, till at last the bishop of Rome by his cunningness succeeded in having the supremacy over them all—so that the Kings of the Earth bowed at his beckoning, making him the vicar of Christ, a God on the earth, and independent in authority, which he really used by oppressing all as far as he could. He confirmed all the old corruptions, and constantly added to the deterioration till the world was filled with all kinds of fraud and idolatry. At Rome anti-Christ is of age, the chief Lord with its triple crown on its head. But as the lording the conscience is anti Christ in all places, the same kind of an oppressor is anti Christ also in the most abject house of worship as a poor infant on the breast, for the conscience is God's throne, and whoever seeks to usurp this throne is anti-Christ. We have already noticed the deterioration of the Christian religion under three heads, viz , the doctrine, the worship and the spirit of Christianity. Whoever desires to know anti-Christ, here is the mark of ignorance in the doctrine, superstition in the worship, and a persecuting spirit. Romanists say that ignorance is the mother of godliness, but God says, "My people are destroyed for lack of knowledge." Hosea 4, 6.

According to this, ignorance is the mother of destruction. Let the professors of Christianity notice the name which shall be in the forehead of the woman—Rev. XVII, 5—it is put in large letters, so that all can read it Mystery, &c. Much is said by men generally of this mystery, and that mystery in religion. But there was no mystery in the religion of Moses. "Those things which are revealed belong to us and to our children " (Deut. 29, 29). And surely there is no mystery in the religion of Jesus Christ. He was the Light of the World, and His doctrine shines as the sun in its own simplicity. It is supposed from this that all who bear some awful mysteries in the religion of Jesus Christ, belong to Babylon—and have the mark of anti Christ. No one doubts the existence of mystery in God, but it is to him it belongs, and there are also mysteries that are incomprehensible in every creature, but they are not a part of religion. There may be many things that are difficult to understand in religion, and yet not mysterious. As the disciple increases in his knowledge of the attributes of God, he becomes better acquainted with the things of God, but as to the mysteries which God has kept to himself, the weakest babe in religion knows as much as the oldest disciple—hence we think that it is a great deterioration in religion for any to undertake to describe the Only Wise God in any form of being that He has not revealed Himself, and to presume to say how God acted n eternity before the worlds were, and how He will act again millions of ages hence. We might think as we hear some preach that their entire religion was before the Book of Genesis and after the Book of Revelation, and oh! how the common people are amazed when they hear such mysteries!! O, such wisdom!! when possibly it is all darkness!! This reminds me of a conversation between two hearers respecting two sermons. "Which was the greatest preacher according to your opinion?" said one. "Mr. ———," said the other. "I am not of the same opinion as you," said the first; "How do you think that he was a greater preacher?" "O," said he, "I understood every word that your preacher said, but as for the other, I did not understand anything he said; he must be a great preacher." There are reasons for fearing that this brother has too many brethren who live on sound, without understanding anything; who weep and rejoice when they hear the word, but after they have gone away from its sound nothing remains. But we will hasten to set before the reader the worst form of all in the deterioration of religion; viz, the mode of supporting it, etc. Here he discusses the tithe or compulsory mode in contradiction to the voluntary mode of the Apostolic Church.

THREE THINGS THAT GOD KEPT TO HIMSELF.

When the Jesuits were urging Stephen, the King of Poland, to persecute the Protestants, he said: "That he durst not; that there were three things that God had kept to Himself—creative power, knowledge of things to come, and authority over the conscience. Hence, he could not but give equal liberty to all his subjects." Many more extracts might be made,* but the above are sufficient to show the chief aim of the magazine.

*See "Literary Essays" (in Welsh), by Rev. L. Edwards, D. D., Bala, Wales.

The Substance of His Two Last Sermons in Wales, Etc.

CHAPTER IV.

The substance of two sermons on the setting apart of John Edwards and Thomas Jones to the eldership office, and Edward Hughes and John Roberts to the deaconship office, in the meeting house of the people, called Baptists in Glynceiriog, July 2d, 1794.

The first sermon on the duties of church officers, and the second on the duties of the people toward their officers, printed by Joseph Tye Wrexham, 1794, price, 3 d. Text, Gal. 5, 13.

The sermons were printed and published at the request of the church at Glynceiriog. He wrote a letter to the said church, signed "M. J. R.," also published.

He also wrote an address to his friends, his children and brethren through all Wales. My translation of which I here give:

Beloved—It may be that this is the last time for me to address you. It is my purpose, if the Lord will, to sail over the ocean soon. I cannot forget the land of my nativity, nor its inhabitants. I am willing to spend and be spent to serve them, and if I shall have life and health and the way open before me, I propose to return and bid well to my brethren, and more joy than this I have not—to hear that my children search continually for the truth and remain steadfast in it. M. J. R.

At the end of the pages of the sermons are variety of notes, many of which are in English for the purpose of inducing young persons who might read them and who are ignorant of the English to acquaint themselves in that language.

Both the sermons and the notes prove that the author was a man of extensive reading and knowledge, and well versed in the holy scriptures.

He published and sent forth a solemn address to the Welsh, calling upon and encouraging them to establish Welsh schools, to teach poor children to read their bibles, etc.

The address is well written and very pathetic, giving an account too of what a vast amount of good has been done in that way by Mrs.

Bevan, of Langhorne, Dr. Stonehouse and Thomas Jones, Esq. It was by their efforts 297,121 were taught to read their bibles during the short time of thirty-nine years.

Besides he published a pamphlet on the "Plan of Supporting Religion in the United States of America," together with a brief description of Kentucky, and sufficient reasons to justify such as to go from this country to America, and a counsel to the Welsh, by Morgan ab Joan Rhees. This must have been a very interesting pamphlet especially at that time. I recollect having heard by an aged minister, who knew him, of his preaching from Psalms 66, 12, "Man hast caused men to rise over our heads; we went through fire and through water, but Thou broughtest us out into a wealthy place."

In that sermon he used rather strong expressions to those times, such as "The king rides upon our heads;" "The royal family ride upon our heads"; "The Arch-Bishops ride upon our heads;" "The Bishops and the church ecclesiastics ride upon our heads;" "The Peer of the realm and the proprietors of the land ride upon our heads, etc.," but Thou broughtest us out into a wealthy (Welsh, wanting nothing) place. I will soon be in America. He was obliged to escape then, being in danger of being apprehended.

The above from a letter from William Morgan, Holyhead, July 25th, 1860.*

---

*I received the above from Mr. William J. Rhees, Washington, D. C.   J. T. G.

THE ALTAR OF PEACE

Being the Substance of a Discourse

Delivered in the

COUNCIL HOUSE, AT GREENVILLE, JULY 5th, 1795,

Before the Officers of the

AMERICAN ARMY AND MAJOR GENERAL WAYNE

Commander-in-Chief and Minister Plenipotentiary

From the United States

TO TREAT WITH THE INDIAN TRIBES

North-West of the Ohio.

BY MORGAN JOHN RHYS,

To which is prefixed

AN ADDRESS OF THE MISSIONARY SOCIETY

With their Constitution

"I Will Give the Heathen for Thine Inheritance."

PHILADELPHIA.
Printed by Ephraim Conrad.
Price, 12½ cents.
The profits arising from the sale to be applied
to the funds of the society.
1798.

The Altar of Peace.

CHAPTER V.

To the Citizens of the United States:—

The Missionary Society of Philadelphia, impressed with the importance of ameliorating the condition and augmenting the happiness of mankind, are impelled by motives of religion and benevolence to attempt the propagation of Christian and civil knowledge among the aborigines of America. Those who have experienced the blessed effects of real religion must feel a desire to disseminate its principles wherever the footsteps of a fellowman may be found. An opportunity offers for such to evince their sincerity by laboring together in accomplishing the ancient prediction. "The knowledge of the Lord shall cover the earth as the waters do the sea."

Living in an age when the devastations of war teach us to appreciate and extend the blessings of peace, all good and enlightened citizens will concur with us that every step which tends to introduce the arts of civilization among the Indians must be highly favorable to the interest of the United States. The easy access which may be had at present to the different tribes by means of government establishments in various parts of their territory, and their tranquil state and the friendly disposition of some of their chiefs dispose the society to believe that their address is not premature. They presume that nothing more is necessary to excite the attention and secure the support of their fellow-citizens than to present their plan to the consideration of the public. The subscribers penetrated with the conviction that their duty and happiness are involved in promoting the knowledge, and in diffusing the spirit of the Christian religion, do associate for the purpose of supporting a missionary among the American heathen and the frontier settlements of the United States, as an eligible mean of accomplishing so desirable an object. Aware of the pernicious effects of party spirit, they think it necessary to adopt for their guide (as well as to exhibit to the world, the principles by which they will be governed) the following constitution:

I. The association shall be called Missionary Society.

II. Any person signing the constitution and paying the sum of one dollar to the treasurer, and the further sum of one dollar yearly is a member during the payment of his or her subscription.

III. The Society shall elect by ballot an acting committee to consist of a treasurer, secretary and seven members, one-third of whom shall be renewed every six months—five shall form a quorum to transact business and have power to call special meetings.

IV. The society shall meet every three months at an appointed place to enact the necessary laws, and deliberate on the reports of the committee respecting the state and progress of the institution.

V. No missionary shall be considered qualified who is not capable of practicing or teaching some useful art as well as a rational system of religion. No other test shall be required excepting evidences of piety and zeal; that he renounces all sectarian names and adopt simply that of Christian.

VI. Should the funds of the Society permit, institutions of instructing the Indians in the agricultural and mechanical arts shall be established among them.

VII. As soon as a sufficient number have subscribed, the committee shall publish under their inspection a periodical miscellany entitled, "Missionary,"* and the profits arising from the sale shall be applied to the funds of the Society.

No alteration or amendment shall be made without the consent of two-thirds of the members, and every such improvement must be proposed three months prior to its discussion. The constitution is left for signature at 177 S. Second street (Philadelphia). February 2d, 1798.

---

*The above periodical was to consist of forty eight pages—large octavo, and to be published at 30 cents a number or $3 a year. The subscribers were to send their names to William Griffiths, Bookseller, 177 South Second street, Philadelphia. (See "Altar of Peace," last page). Does any one know whether any issues of the above periodical were published? J. T. G.

A Sermon.

"Then Gideon built an altar thereunto the Lord and called it Jehovah Sallum ; i. e., the Lord give Peace." Judges VI, 24

A noble example for all generals and commanders of armies! Gideon, when going out to war, erected an altar to the God of Peace. His object was not devastation and plunder, but to defend the lives, liberty and property of his brethren. When these objects were obtained, the sword was sheathed and he returned to his occupation, crowned with honor. Gideon, as a worshiper of God, is worthy of imitation by all men, if there be a first cause, a disposer of events, a distributor of rewards and punishments—he is certainly an object of adoration. Some have supposed man to be a religious animal, that it is religion and not reason which distinguishes him from the beast; but without the exercise of reason, I am at a loss to know how we are to prove the existence of the Almighty. It is true in most countries, savage as well as civilized, we meet with the temple and the priest, the altar and the offering, the mythology of the heathen, the mosques of Mahomet, the superstitions of popery, the circumscribed ceremonies of the Jews—all have a tendency to prove that there is such a thing as real religion. Let us search for it, not by rejecting wholly everything that bears the appearance of religion, but by acting the part of the bee, extract the honey from every flower.

Although the Western World be a wilderness, we meet here with abundance of flowers which would adorn the most beautiful garden in Europe. Shall we reject those valuable productions of the earth because they grow in an uncultivated soil ? Surely not. Shall we then reject the noble precepts of Christ, and despise His institutions, because they have been obscured by the weeds of popery and Mahometanism ? God forbid! Rather let us cut down the groves of Baal and despise his worship. Let us reject every hypothesis that will not bear the test of examination; let us believe nothing but what is supported by evidence, and may be proved by reason that religion is certainly rational, which represents the Supreme Being in the most amiable manner, rewards virtue, punishes vice, publishes peace to the penitent, unites man to man and all good men to God. Such is the Christian religion in its primitive simplicity. Although its advocates are engaged in the most important war, a war with ignorance and vice, yet, after the example of Gideon, they continually pray for peace. The Commander-in-Chief has ordered them to publish peace in every house they enter—peace to the Indians, to Europe, Asia, Africa and America. Their commission is to preach the Gospel to every creature, to proclaim glory to God in the highest, on earth peace, good will towards men. However, if we wish to enjoy a permanent peace in the world, the private circle or the conscience, the Bible declares we must cease to do evil and learn to do good. The rule is short, and the commandments are easy. All the precepts of Jehovah center in one syllable—Love. The laws and the prophets, like the rays of the sun collected to a focus, here shine and burn. The man who loves God as the supreme good, and his neighbor as himself, surmounts every obstruction with ease, because he is borne above earth on the wings of love; the philanthropist is every person's neighbor, the White, the Black and the Red are alike to him; he recognizes in each a brother, a child of the same common parent, an heir of immortality, and a fellow traveler to eternity. He knows how to make allowance for the prejudices of nations and individuals; instead of declaiming and tyranizing, he endeavors to lead (with the cords of love and the bands of men) all his fellowmen to think, and judge for themselves, what is right. Having done this, the foundation is laid for a glorious fabric! the man who dares to think seriously for himself brings a complete sacrifice to the altar of peace; his ear receives instructions, the memory receives information, the judgment discerns between truth and error, his eye or principle is fixed on the glory of God and the public good, and his feet or affections persevere in the path which leads to immortal blessedness. Brethren, where we have fallen short in any duty, especially that of gratitude, let us move on with a firm and steady step in the great work of reformation, and as we are surrounded by temptations, let us combat the powers of darkness and the enemy will flee before us; with the weapons of eternal truth let us fight the foe, and our rallying point shall be the Altar of Peace. Permit me to descend to particulars, and apply the subject to the pending treaty, the Lord give Peace. But, sirs! in order to establish a durable peace some sacrifices must be made on both sides. The love of conquest and enlargement of territory should be sacrificed—every nation or tribe having an indefeasible right of soil, as well as a right to govern themselves in what manner they think proper, for which reason the United States purchase the right of soil from the Indians. Self interest and avarice, being the root of all evil, ought to be sacrificed as a burnt offering, for the good of mankind. The desire of revenge should be immediately offered on the altar of forgiveness, although thy brother trangress against thee seventy times seven in a day. Dissimulation and intrigue, with every species of deceptive speculation and fraudulent practice, ought to be sacrificed on the altars of strict honor and inflexible justice. In short, as the Altar of Peace is our text,

34

the sermon on our future conduct should be, "Do Justice and Love Mercy." Tell the Indians they must "go and do likewise;" inform them that righteousness is the parent of peace, foreign and domestic; that without it there can be no tranquility in the nation, the neighborhood, or in the bosom of the individual. Endeavor, therefore, by all possible means to instill a just knowledge of this principle into their minds, for it must precede universal peace Why did the prophet say, "They shall not hurt nor destroy?" Because, first, "the knowledge of God shall cover the earth as the waters cover the sea."

If we were to form any idea of the signs of the times, the day of universal knowledge, peace and happiness cannot be at any great distance It will advance upon us like the rising sun, whose light irresistibly spreads far and wide. But do not imagine that we are to be idle spectators. God carries on his work by means, and employs rational instruments, and as we are at present in an Indian country, we should devise and adopt the most likely measures to civilize the savage tribes. We have an opportunity of knowing something of their disposition. If peace can be amicably concluded, much may be done, but we are not to forget the natural grades from a savage state to that of civilization. I am clearly of the opinion that rational preachers ought to be employed to remove their ancient superstition, give them just notions of the Great Spirit, and teach them rules of moral rectitude I am aware that something more is wanted. Unless husbandry and the mechanical arts be introduced with those missionaries, they will never be able to prevail on them to quit their ancient customs and manners. Government should therefore interfere and assist. That good may be done by individuals none can deny—the Moravian Indians are a convincing proof of it. Still, their laudable efforts will be ineffectual to bring over the great body of the people without further aid, and a general intercourse between them and virtuous men.

'Tis to be lamented that the frontiers of America have been peopled in many places by men of bad morals. I do not mean by this to throw a disagreeable reflection upon all the frontier inhabitants, for I know there are many virtuous characters among them, but certain it is that there are a great number of white, as well as red savages. It will therefore be necessary to have such communications with the different tribes as to convince them of the good will of the Americans in general. If at the conclusion of this treaty some interchanges of persons could take place between the United States and the different tribes, so that some Americans might have their residence in the Indian towns, and the Indians in like manner, reside in some of the principal towns on the frontiers, it might be the means of terminating all future differences without war; of cultivating harmony and friendship among the tribes;

of bringing offenders on both sides to justice, and causing treaties to be respected throughout the different nations. If such a system could be introduced cultivation and instruction would naturally follow and the Americans and Indians would become one people, and have but one interest at heart—the good of the whole That such a thing should take place is certainly desirable Let us, therefore, in the first place, follow the example of Gideon by erecting an altar, and offer the necessary sacrifices to obtain peace; let us by acts of righteousness and deeds of mercy make that peace permanent; let every probable means be made use of to enlighten the poor heathens, that they may quit their childish and cruel customs, and add to their love of liberty and hospitality, piety, industry, mechanical and literary acquirements; let us join them in prayer that the "Great Spirit" may enlighten their eyes and purify their hearts, give them a clear sky and smooth water, guard them against the bad birds, and remove the briars from their paths; protect them from the dogs of war, which are ever exciting them to acts of barbarous cruelty, that they may never attend to their barking, but continue to keep the bloody hatchet in the ground and smoke the calumet of peace until its odors perfume the air."

Sweet Peace! source of joy, parent of plenty, promoter of commerce and manufactures, nurse of arts and agriculture, angelic Peace! Could I but set forth thy amiable qualities, who would but love thee? O, daughter of Heaven, first offspring of the God of Love, hasten to make thy residence with us on earth!

P. S.—The above has been copied from the original pamphlet, which is in the Bucknell Library of Crozer Theological Seminary, Chester, Pa.

A Sermon by the Celebrated Morgan John Rhees.

CHAPTER VI.

MEN AND BRETHREN:—

Another year having been numbered among those which cannot be recalled, and many of our friends and acquaintance in the same year, having gone that journey—"From whose bourne no traveller returns," a variety of useful reflections might be made on the occasion. Indeed it is not probable that all of us who are now present shall see a similar anniversary. Like leaves in Autum, we wither and drop from the tree of life. "To the house appointed for all living" we are borne on the wings of time. Let us then be admonished to think of our latter end. "To number our days and apply our hearts to the attainment of wisdom." To devote the short period we may have to live to the service of our God, our country and the whole human family. We have now assembled for the purpose of public worship. Every worship presupposes a belief in the existence, the excellency and perfection of the adored object. "He that cometh to God must not only believe that he is, but that he is a rewarder of those who seek him." "The fool hast said in his heart, there is no God." "The fool also maketh a mock of sin." Shall we, because fools say there is no God and make a mock of sin, reject the convictions of our own consciences? We should however observe that it was in his "his heart" the fool said "no God." To speak this openly and publish it to the world might not suit his interest or it might require more ingenuity, and better information to defend a system so absurd in its principles and destructive in its tendency. The theory and practice of men are often at variance. Some theoretic atheists may live what is termed a moral life, but practical atheists (who are by no means few in number) declare in their hearts, that is by their actions that they at least wish there was no God. Theoretic atheism has comparatively but few advocates. It verily requires a high degree of refinement in false philosophy to banish altogether from the mind a belief in the existence of a "First Cause." (a). It is a belief which is common to all nations—savages as well as civilized. Man as it were by instinct, or rather a divine principle implanted in his mind breathes after immorality, and at every occurence of distress or of danger cries out: "Oh, my God!" This he has done in every age, and in every clime when or whenever man has departed from the worship of the "One true and Living God." It is because his faculties have been deranged by corruption; it is because he has ceased to exist after the image of his Creator that he has made to himself gods after his own image. The more degraded man became in his character; his gods became proportionably abominable. Still he retained a belief in some divinity. Consequently the impressions of a "first cause" were not altogether effaced from his mind. This indeed would be a difficult task while the book of nature continued open before him; while all things visible declare a commencement and origin; while the wonderful machinery of the universe continue to take their perpetual rounds without disorder or confusion; while no new order of animals or beings make their appearance among us—"Nature in all places of her dominion" will cry aloud—"A God! A God!" has created, preserves and governs the universe. Yes, the truth is engraved in characters so legible in the Heavens above, the earth beneath, the waters under—every animate and inanimate substance, but especially on the faculties of the human soul—"that he who runs may read." It is true, that many, too many instead of embracing truth as we find it on the surface of all created objects, as its links are connected in the great chain of harmonies and consonances through the wide and extensive field of nature, bewilder their brains, puzzle and obscure their faculties with the eternity of matter, the doctrines of chance, and the fortuity of atoms! By endeavoring to solve every mystery to the standard of their own depraved reason, and to admit of nothing as true but what can be explained with mathematical precision, they attempt to dethrone God and establish their own almighty reason in his seat. "Professing themselves to be wise they have become fools." "For the invisible things of God from the creation of the world are clearly seen being understood by the things that are made—even His eternal power and Godhead." Having said thus much of the existence of Jehovah, it may not be amiss to observe as a farther preliminary towards the elucidation of our subject; that the history of all nations represent mankind as corrupt and depraved creatures that from whatever sources this evil had its origin. Its existence cannot be denied—that different nations attribute the calamity to different causes; that the Hebrews are the only people who have given us a clear and distinct view of the subject, and that it appears from the fitness of things far more improbable that the Almighty should have created man and then leave him to himself without any rule for his conduct than that he should give him a decree and a test of his obedience.

In a book emphatically styled the Scriptures we find the apostacy of man fully explained, the consequence of his fall awfully pronounced, and his recovery from that state wonderfully exhibited. Of the authenticity of the Scriptures or writings, the evidence, external and internal which accompany them, are the best testimony of their being a revelation from God. One thing is certain, that without such a record, mankind would have forever groped in the dark, respecting the knowledge of their origin and destiny. Besides the experience of all ages has fully evinced the necessity of some Superior Instructor to the weak and uncertain light of reason. (b). It was worthy of "The Father of Light from Whom proceedeth every good and perfect" gift to give such an Instructor. "God, Who at sundry times and in divers manners, spake in times unto our fathers by the prophets" and other means suitable to His dignity "Has spoken unto us by His Son." We proceed then to prove that the Christ spoken of in our text is "The Son of the Living God." That such an extraordinary person as Christ was born at Bethlehem lived and preached among the Jews and was crucified at Jerusalem. Several Pagan writers as well as the Disciples testify that a great light or a new star appeared in the East which directed the wise men to the place of His birth is recorded by Chalcidius; that Herod the King of Palestine made a great slaughter of innocent children among others than his own sons is mentioned by Macrobius, as a known fact and that the Roman Emperor on hearing this news, should have said, "He had rather be one of Herod's hogs than his son;" that Jesus had been taken by His parents to Egypt is acknowledged by Celsus, who said that He had learned the arts of magic in that country; that He was condemned and crucified under a Pontius Pilate is recorded by Tacitus, and that Pilate himself communicated a history of the event to Tiberius appears evident from the references made to it by the early writers; that there was a miraculous darkness and a great earthquake at the time of our Saviour's death is attested by Phlegon. But what need we dwell on a point not much disputed. Those who believe there were such persons as Augustus and Tiberius Cæsar, must by the same kind of testimony believe there was such a person as Jesus Christ. The burden of the proof before us is to show that Christ was the Son of God in a unique or more excellent manner than any other person ever could, or can be; that He was the Messiah—"The only Begotten of the Father, full of Grace and Truth." This we will endeavor to prove by the miracles which Christ wrought by the coincidence of the predictions related in Ancient Scriptures with His life, sufferings, death and resurrection. By the accomplishments of predictions which He delivered, the doctrines and precepts which He taught and the success which attended the first preaching of his gospel. That miracles were wrought by Christ is admitted by many of his adversaries. Celsus, Julian the Apostate and Porphyry (who were among the principal opposers of Christianity) had no other refuge when contending with Christians but to attribute them to the art of magic. The inveterate and malicious Jews in a similar manner to Beelzebub, the prince of devil—so far both parties agree that miracles were wrought. The facts indeed were too stubborn to be denied. Everything was done openly before the eyes of the public where every person had an opportunity of investigating and examining into the merits of the case. Deception, the most refined, could never have assimilated itself with such things. Thousands fed with a few loaves; the blind receiving their sight; 'the deaf having their hearing restored by a word; the lame leaping like a hart; the dead brought to life and even quitting their graves were miracles not to be conjured by Magi nor the prowell of his infernal majesty. In every instance where miracles have been pretended by magicians or others independent of the delusions attending them their powers have been limited and have fallen short of "the finger of God." In Egypt, the Magi in some instances imitated the miracles of Moses. In others they could not, declaring that "the finger of God was there" * * * that these miracles of Christ were of God is evident from their nature, kind and tendency. They were all worthy of a benovelent Being and manifested His power. The sick, afflicted and distressed were the principal objects of them, and if the dead were to be raised it was partly to soothe and allay the grief of the living. Altogether dissimilar to pretended miracles and legerdemain tricks; they were both useful and permanent in their effect. Several of the subjects of them outlined the person who performed them.

If any adverse power could have performed similar miracles, no doubt it would have been done to discredit Christianity. The disciples of the devil were not equal to the task. The evil spirits fled from the presence of Jesus, confessing Him to be "the Christ of God." Independent of revelation the probability is strong that wicked and malignant spirits have an existence in our world, and that they have more influence in the affairs of men than many are willing to admit. So far as the consent of all nations and ages go to prove anything, it is in favor of this belief. But as without microscopes we should never have discovered numerous tribes of insects, which inhabit our earth, so without the light of revelation we cannot ascertain what spirits are and act in the region of our air. The Scriptures assure us that angels, both good and bad, are conversant in this world, and that more of them should make their appearance in the days of our Saviour than at any other period is not at all surprising. One object of His mission appears to be to unfold the mysteries of the invisible world, so far as they were connected with the interest of mankind. To demonstrate the power of God, in His own person; by making it manifest to all, even the weakest capacity; that though there existed a powerful and wicked spirit, that He was nevertheless under the control and government of the Almighty; that although He might inflict diseases, and otherwise distress the human family, He was still subject to the will of Heaven—and even under the imperious necessity of fleeing from the faithful followers of Christ, whenever they resisted His temptations, the miracles performed upon the demoniacs may then be defended, though no such possessions are now observed among mankind.(d) Our argument, however, rests on miracles in general, and though this point is warmly disputed as being contrary to the order of nature—the laws of matter and motion—we trust that every candid mind will acknowledge that the author of nature may govern and direct the machine, He formed in such a manner as to Him appears best adapted to the good of His creatures. The laws of gravity are often suspended by the influence of magnetism and electricity and why may the Creator and preserver of all things not suspend, change or infringe upon the common order of things whenever He thinks it proper to produce extraordinary effects evidently tending to His own honor and the good of His offspring? It does not follow because a thing has happened ten thousand times or even a million of times that it never has failed, nor even can fail. Those who declare that they have met with contrary appearances in certain cases, testify what they have seen and why may their evidence not be true. Magnetism and electricity were once as incredible to the multitude as the Gospel miracles, yet the award of a sufficient number of credible witnesses have established those facts, however contrary to received notions. There are phenomenas in nature not yet accounted for and notwithstanding the great advances made in natural knowledge, we are not certain that they are all reducible to the laws of matter and motion. The only safe rule in such cases is to abide by the award of credible testimonies, however contrary to received notions and analogies. If that course of nature or series of events which follow each other in the order of cause and effect we are ignorant of what may be the divine purposes and appointments of secret causes, and the corresponding variety of events, that we can only appeal to the facts, to credible relations of what actually has been, in order to know the course of nature. The Scripture miracles may not be contrary to its fixed principles and immutability. Since the course of nature understood in a popular sense, falls so short of the true course of nature as here defined, i. e., as admitting the instrumentality of beings superior to us—men divinely inspired, good angels, evil spirits and many other influences, of which our present philosophy can take no cognizance with respect to moral analogy. Though the case is somewhat different, it is sufficient to say that God is infinite; that natural and revealed religion are in all principal things most wonderfully analogous, and that as far as moral analogy carries weight with it, there is positive evidence for the Scripture miracles. In common affairs a great number of credible evidence amounts to an absolute certainty, and what evidence for common facts have ever exceeded those for the Scripture miracles? If we place this subject upon another footing, i. e., the order of nature as it respects the human mind, we shall discover "that a man's thoughts, words and actions are all generated by something previous." There is an established course for these things, an analogy of which every man is a judge, from what he feels in himself and sees in others; and to suppose any number of men, in determinate circumstances, to vary from this general tenor of human nature in like circumstances, is a miracle and may be made a miracle of any magnitude, i. e., incredible to any degree, by increasing the number and magnitude of the deviations. It is therefore a miracle in the human mind as great as any can be conceived in the human body to suppose that infinite multitudes of Christians, Jews and heathen in the primitive times, should have borne such unquestionable testimony to the miracles said to be performed by Christ and His Apostles upon the human body, unless they were really performed. In like manner, the reception which the miracles recorded in the Old Testament met with, is a miracle unless those miracles were true. The very existence of the works of the Old and the New Testaments of the Jewish and Christian religions, &c, &c, are miracles unless we allow the Scripture miracles. Here, then, a man must either deny an analogy and association and become an absolute sceptic, or acknowledge that very strong analogies may sometimes be violated, i. e., he must have recourse to something miraculous, to something supernatural, according to his narrow views.

The next question then will be, which of the two opposite miracles will agree best with all his other notions; whether it be more analogous to the nature of God, Providence, the allowed history of the world, the known progress of man in this life, &c, &c, to suppose that God imparted to certain select persons of eminent piety the power of working miracles; or to suppose that he confounded the understandings, affections and whole train of associations, of entire nations, so as that men who in all other things seem to have been conducted like other men, should in respect of the history of Christ, the Prophets and Apostles, act in a manner repugnant to all our ideas and experiences. Now, as this last supposition cannot be maintained at all upon the footing of Deism, so it would be but just as probable as the first, even though the objector should deny the possibility of the being of a God." For the least presumption that there may be a being of immense or infinite power, knowledge and goodness, immediately turns the scale in favor of the first supposition." "If any one should affirm or think, as some persons seem to do, that a miracle is impossible, let him consider that this is denying God's omnipotence, and even maintaining that man is the supreme agent in the universe " We might farther observe (if enough had not been said already) that most of the Scripture miracles, though nearly related, are independent of each other—that anyone of them being proved true diminishes the objections to others—that the credulity which has been too common in false miracles cannot be accounted for unless many true ones had been wrought; that the accomplishment of prophecy by implying a miracle, provided events which have already happened can be proved to have been foretold in Scripture in a manner exceeding chance, and human foresight, must remove the objections to miracles.

We proceed then to prove from ancient predictions, "That Jesus is the Christ, the Son of the Living God," and as the source from whence the testimony is taken is disputed by some to be genuine. We shall occasionally defend the original as well as the application, that Moses wrote the Pentateuch, or five fold volume. We have the same evidence as that Homer wrote the Iliad, i. e., The Consent of the Learned in all Ages. Plato, Polesnus, Artapanus, Pythagoras, Theopompus and Disdoius Siculus place him in the front of six of the most ancient lawgivers; thus—Moses, Lanchius, Sesonchosis, Barhoris Amasis and Darius, father of Xerxes. Tho' there are no people at present living after the laws of Lycurgus and Solon, we have no just reason to disbelieve that those founders of the Lacedemonian and Athenian governments did not write such laws, for every nation is supposed to be a faithful depository of its own rule of conduct. What reason then can be urged against the authenticity of the Books of Moses when an entire nation even to this day receive them as genuine? The history of the creation, deluge, etc , might have been brought down by four persons to the days of Moses. Methusaleh lived with Adam 243 years; Shem, the son of Noah, with Methusaleh about 97 years; Jacob, with Shem, 50 years; Joseph lived 71 years after his father and brethren came to Egypt, so that Amram, the father of Moses, might not only see Joseph, but Moses might have conversed with his grandfather, Koath, who had seen Jacob. Is it possible then that the Book of Genesis could have been forged and imposed upon a people who from their own knowledge of facts might have immediately detected the imposture? When in consequence of iniquity the age of man was shortened it became necessary in order to preserve the knowledge and worship of the one true God to have a written law. That such a law was given to Hebrews is evident from its reception by that people ever since their Exodus out of Egypt. Their judges, prophets, historians and reformers have had constant reference to it in all their writings unless the Divine authority of those laws had been established beyond the possibility of doubt. Is it probable that any people should have submitted to such heavy burdens as they enjoined? In point of human policy some of the laws were apparently absurd. Such was the law which ordained that all the males should appear three times a year in one place to worship on their solemn festivities, thus leaving a defenceless nation of women and children to shift for themselves against surrounding enemies. Such, however, is the fact, and such were the effects of this law that while the Jews obeyed it an enemy never invaded their coasts. Such, also, are the facts respecting their seventh year in which they were neither to plow, sow or reap—that they lacked nothing. The books annexed to the law of Moses tho' not delivered in so awful and sublime a manner have had a similar reception as it respects their authenticity. Joshua most probably wrote the last chapter of Deuteronium, and Phineas the last verses of the book under his name. The Judges and Ruth were written as it is supposed by Samuel, and the First and Second Samuel by himself, by Nathan and by Gad. These contain the history of the Jews from the year of the world, 2888 to the year, 2987. The Books of Kings written by several of the Prophets, who were generally the Jewish historiographers, extend from 2989 to 3442. The Books of Chronicles recapitulate the history from the beginning of the world to the year 3468. Ezra wrote his history, etc., from 3468 to 3588. Nehemiah continued it from 3550 to 3563. David, whose hymns were sung by the people as a part of their divine service, began to reign in the year 3306. Hosea, Micah and Nahum were co-temporaries with him. Jeremiah began his Prophecy in 3875, and lived at the same time with Zephaniah. Daniel was carried into Babylon in 3401, and prophesied until 3470. Ezekiel prophesied at Babylon in 3590. Malachi seems to have lived until the year, 3589, and Simon, the just, who died about thirty-one years after Alexander the Great, perfected and finally settled the canon of the Jewish Scriptures. In the year, 3727, the Scriptures were translated into the Greek language for the use of the Hellenist or Greek Jews, whom Alexander had planted in Egypt. This translation contributed much to the spread of religious knowledge in the Western parts of the world. For the Jews, their synagogues and worship, were, after Alexander's death, dispersed almost everywhere among the nations. Ptolemy, 320 years before Christ, carried one hundred thousand Jews into Egypt and planted a great number besides in Cyrenalybian.

Seleucus, another of Alexander's succession, 300 years B. C., transplanted an immense number of them, through Cilicia, Lesser and Greater Asia. Everywhere they carried the Scriptures with them, and in a short time the Greek version was commonly and publicly used. This fact alone is sufficient to prove that it was impossible for the Old Testament to have been forged after the birth of Christ. It is evident the books of the Old Testament were in existence. What remains for us is to examine their contents and inquire into the character of their authors, that the Supreme Disposer of events should communicate His will to certain of His creatures more than to others may appear strange to some. "A revelation made to others, say they, are not a revelation to us." "Nor are we obliged to give credit to any such revelation, although it may be attended with such circumstances and testimony as would amply establish the truth of any other fact." The book of nature, we admit, is a revelation to all who will open their eyes to read it. But, surely, there is nothing incredible in the doctrine, that the omniscient God should select His peculiar servants and manifest to them what should afterwards take place. If it should appear that the predictions of ancient prophets have been really accomplished, this will be something like proof that the thing was revealed to them from Heaven. For it is evident that man of himself cannot foretell future events—he may calculate effects from a cause already existing. Having established principles for his rules he may deduce consequences without foreign aid—the prudent will not presume to go farther. As to the prescience of the devil—we know little or nothing about it. He may teach his servants like the celebrated oracles of the heathen, to give evasive answers so that whatever the event might be, the exposition might be made favorable to the oracle. No so the prophecies of Scripture. They have explicitly foretold certain events, which would befall individuals and nations, and that by a minuteness of detail, which, had not the events happened exactly, exactly as described, nothing but contempt could have pursued the authors. No other way has been attempted to evade the accuracy of some of their predictions, but by asserting that their writings were composed after the events had taken place. This objection we have already obviated by the chronology of their lives. Besides, it is unfortunate for the objector that many of the predictions were fulfilled in the lifetime of the predictor, and those who were not, have been so faithfully preserved on record that the hands of tyrants and of time have not been able to destroy them.

The Jewish oracles or predictions might be divided into four classes: to the foretelling of events nigh at hand, to others more remote, to such as had respect to the whole Hebrew nations, and to such as regarded only foreign nations. Of the former kind we have a great number of instances—such as the advancement of Joshua, the conquest of Palestine, the victory of Barak, the advancement and rejection of Saul, the elevation of David, the revolt of Absalom, the advancement of Jeroboam and the separation of the ten tribes, the exemplary punishment of Ahab and Jezebel, the miseries and death of Jehoiakim, etc., etc. Of those more remote we have the predictions of Moses, respecting the several captivities of the Israelites as well as their present scattered and exile state. The punishment inflicted on the rebuilder of Jerico foretold by Joshua 570 years before it took place; the destruction of Jerusalem by Nebuchadnezzar foretold by several of the prophets; Isaiah's prediction of Cyrus by name, as a resorer of liberty to the Jews; of the manner Antiochus Epiphanes would treat the Hebrews and how he should be punished for his cruelties, and a variety of others.

Those which respect the Jews as a nation are everywhere to be found in their writings from the pilgrimage of their Patriarchs to the last of their Kings, and their existence as a body politic, and as of necessity, they had connections with other nations. Their prophets have foretold, as if they had lived on the spot, the fate of other empires—such as the ruin of Egypt and Tyre, under Nebuchadnezzar; also of the Mobites, under the same king, after they had subsisted as a nation almost fourteen years; the destruction of Niniveh and its empire, of Babylon under Cyrus, of the Persian Empire by Alexander; of the manner the prince conquered a great part of the world, and of the division of his empire into four kingdoms, etc., etc. Many reflection might be made on the above predictions, as corroborative evidence in favor of what we are more especially to prove, i. e., that the prophecies of the Old Testament evince that Jesus is "The Christ, the Son of the Living God."

We shall, however, waive this argument and proceed to quote such passages as in our opinion are applicable to Christ, and to Him only. By the oracle or voice of God in Eden, Christ is styled, "The Seed of the Woman, Who Should Bruise the Serpent's Head." This declaration of the Almighty, at the same time it displayed His sovereignty and goodness, laid the foundation of a new religion, suitable to the fallen condition of man. The conduct and expectations of Patriarchs and Prophets fully evinces that this was the ground work of their hope. They all expected a Messiah who should bruise the old serpent's head and destroy the works of the devil. Believing in Him who was to come though yet "invisible." "They saluted the promise and entered into rest." However, obscure the promise might be to our first parents, they certainly considered it of greater import, than that one of their offspring should knock a snake on the head, and that, at the expense of being himself—bit on the heel.

The promise to Abraham is more explicit. "In thy seed shall the nations of the earth be blessed." It does not speak of seeds as many, but is confined to one, namely—"Christ;" for who besides Him has united in one church—the whole family of believers from every nation under Heaven. "The sceptre," said Jacob, "Shall not depart from Judah, nor a lawgiver from between his feet, until Shiloh come, and to him shall the gathering of the people be." This prophecy evinces three things: 1. That the sceptre was to be established in the tribe of Judah, before the Shiloh should make his appearance. 2. That the sceptre was to give way to an inferior dignity which the Patriarch sets forth by the word "lawgiver" which was the case after the overthrow of the Jewish Monarchs. 3. There was a necessity that this last dignity should also come to an end, which did not take place till the advancement of Herod the Great to the throne of Judea.

The general tax in the days of Augustus, when Joseph and Mary went to their own village, Bethlehem, to be registered, is a convincing proof of the sovereignty of the Romans at that time. This is confirmed by several Roman historians as Tacitus, Suetonius and Dion, that the Messiah should be born at Bethlehem, of the family of David is expressly foretold. "But thou Bethlehem Ephratah, though thou be little among the thousands of Israel, yet out of thee shall he come forth unto me, that is to be ruler in Israel, whose goings forth have been from of old from the days of eternity." "There I will make the horn of David to bud. I have ordained a lamp for mine anointed. His enemies I will clothe with shame, but upon himself shall his crown flourish." "And there shall come forth a rod out of the stem of Jesse, and a branch shall grow out of his roots and the Spirit of the Lord shall rest upon him." This stem of Jesse is also styled "the root of Jesse," "the root and offspring of David who should stand for an ensign of the people to whom the gentiles should seek and whose rest shall be glorious." That Christ should be born of a Virgin in a miraculous manner is strongly implied in the promise already cited. He was emphatically "the seed of the woman." "Behold," saith Isaiah, "a Virgin shall conceive and bear a son, and shall call his name Immanuel, God with us." This is a sign promised by the Lord Himself to confound the Israelites who wearied Him with their iniquities. That a Virgin should conceive and bear a son in the ordinary way could be neither a sign nor excite astonishment. But the birth of Christ was both a sign and a miracle. The interpretation of the Septuagint is strictly conformable to this application of the prophecy, and the first opposition to it as such was made by Symmachus in the second century. That the Messiah was to be born before the dissolution of the Jewish state, and the destruction of the second temple is clearly predicted by Daniel, Haggai and Zechariah. Daniel says, Chapter IX, "Seventy weeks are determined upon thy people and upon thy Holy City to finish the transgression, and to make an end of sins, and to make reconciliation for iniquity, and to bring in everlasting righteousness, and to seal up the vision and prophecy, and to anoint the Most Holy. Know therefore and understand that from the going forth of the commandment to restore and build Jerusalem unto the Messiah, the Prince shall be seven weeks and three score and two weeks, and after the three score and two week shall Messiah be cut off, but not for Himself. And the people of the Prince shall come, shall destroy the city and the sanctuary, and the end thereof shall be with a flood, and unto the end of the of the war desolations are determined.

And He shall confirm the covenant with many for one week, and in the midst of the week He shall cause the sacrifice and oblation to cease, and for the overspreading abomination, he shall make it desolate even until the consummation, and that determined shall be poured on the desolate. It may be necessary to observe that the prophetic week is put for seven years, and that the prophet writing in Chaldea, takes the Chaldean year for his data, which consisted of 360 days. Whoever will take the trouble to compute the weeks of Daniel, will find that they have been exactly accomplished, both as it respects the birth and death of Christ, the destruction of the second temple, and the desolation which followed. With respect to the language of the Prophets and the completion of their predictions, the enquirer after truth, would do well to consult that lucid Commentator, Sir Isaac Newton. The second prediction which we shall quote under this head, is that of Haggai, who expressly informs us that the Messiah was to appear during the second Temple which was begun to be built by the order of Cyrus, finished under Darius, son of Hystaspes, and destroyed by Vespasius. "And I will shake all nations and the desire of all nations shall come, and I will fill this house with glory saith the Lord of Hosts. "The glory of this latter house shall be greater than the former, saith the Lord of Hosts, and in this place will I give peace saith the Lord of Hosts." This prophecy speaks of a great change in the political world, such as had taken place by the conquests of the Romans, previous to the coming of our Saviour.

It describes the Messiah as the expectation of the Gentiles, agreeable to the idea given of him to Abraham. It fixes the period of his appearance during the existence of the Temple built by Zerubba-

bel, and makes the glory of that house to depend upon its being
honored with the presence of Christ. Zechariah represents the coming of the Messiah as near at hand, while Balaam almost ten ages
before intimated His coming at a considerable distance. "I see him
but not nigh." Malachi also said: "The Lord whom ye seek shall
suddenly come to His Temple, even the messenger of the covenant
whom ye delight in. Behold He shall come saith the Lord of Hosts!
That there was a general expectations of such a person as Christ is
evident from the writings of Heathens as well as the calculations of the
Jews. It is true the latter, after they had rejected their true Messiah,
fixed their calculations at the expiration of the seventy weeks which
was the third year after the death of Christ.

The reason of their being deluded by so many false Messiahs, that
Jesus Christ was to fill the important offices of Prophet, Priest and
King appears from the following predictions: "I will raise them up",
says God by Moses, "A Prophet from among their brethren, like
unto thee, and will put my words in His mouth, and He shall speak
unto them all that I shall command Him. And it shall come to pass
that whosoever will not hearken unto My words which He shall
speak in My name, I will require it of Him." "Search the Scriptures" says Christ, "for in them ye think ye have eternal life, and they
are they which testify of Me." "For had ye believed Moses, ye would
have believed Me, for he wrote of Me. But if ye believe not his writings,
how shall ye believe My words?" "The resemblances between Moses
and Christ wherein they differed, and where the latter excelled are well
drawn by the writers of the New Testament. "Moses, as a faithful
servant, and Christ, as a Son," fulfilled the work assigned to them by
the Father of the Universe. If Moses was King in Jeshurun, Christ
was established a "King over His Holy Hill of Zion." His Kingdom
indeed, was very different from what the Jews expected, being "not
of this world," and His priesthood dissimilar to that of Aaron, being,
"according to the order of Melchisedec an eternal priesthood." The
particulars respecting the life, sufferings, death, resurrection and
character of Chirst are so clearly described by the Ancient Prophets
that some of the Jewish Rabbis have been driven to the necessity of
inventing a double Messiah, "One who was to redeem them, and
another who was to suffer for them; the one to precede, fight and
suffer death; the other to conquer, reign and never die. "This con-
cession is certainly favorable to the Christians, for it admits of a suffering Messiah." Who indeed can read the 22d Psalm and the 53d
chapter of Isaiah without admitting it, and also the application of the
prophecy to Christ. Was He not "a man of sorrow and acquainted
with grief?" "Surely He hath borne our griefs and carried our sor-

rows. He was wounded for our transgressions; He was bruised for our iniquities; the chastisement of our peace was upon Him, and with His stripes we are healed. He is brought as a lamb to the slaughter, and a sheep before her shearers is dumb -He opened not His mouth. He was taken away by distress and judgement; He was cut off from the land of the living, for the transgression of my people was He stricken. And He made His grave with the rich in His death. because He had done no violence, neither was any deceit in His mouth.

The circumstantial accomplishment of this prophecy cannot be denied. Let us see how the other Prophets correspond with Isaiah, and if we join the Prophets and Evangelists together, it will appear the Messiah was to suffer which Christ hath suffered. If Zechariah says: "They weighed for my price thirty pieces of silver;" Matthew will shew that Judas sold Jesus for "thirty pieces of silver." If Isaiah says: "That He was wounded;" if Zechariah: "They shall look on me whom they have pierced;" if the Prophet David: "They pierced my hand and my feet;" the Evangelists will show how He was fastened to the cross, and Jesus Himself, "the print of the nails." If the Psalmist informs us, "They should laugh him to scorn, and shake their heads, saying: He trusted in the Lord that he would deliver Him, Matthew will describe the same action and the same expression, "For they that passed by reviled Him, wagging their heads and saying: He trusted in God, let Him deliver Him now if He will have Him, for He said I am the Son of God. Let David say, "my God, my God, why hast Thou forsaken me? And the son of David will shew in whose person David spoke it—"Eli, Eli, Lama Sabbacthani?" Let Isaiah say, "He was numbered with the transgressors" and you shall find Him crucified between two thieves, one on His right and the other on His left. Read in the Psalmist—"In my thirst, they gave Me vinegar to drink." "Jesus, that the Scriptures might be fulfilled said, I thirst, and they took a sponge and filled it with vinegar and put it on a reed and gave Him to drink." Read farther yet—"They put my garment among them, and cast lots upon my vesture, and to fulfill the prediction the soldiers shall make good the distinction," who took his garments and made four parts, and also His coat. Now the coat was without a seam, woven from the top throughout. They said, therefore, let us not rend it, but cast lots for it, whose it be.

The resurrection of Christ, a point on which the faith and hope of all believers rest is thus foretold by David: "I foresaw the Lord always before my face, for He is on my right hand, that I should not be moved. Therefore did my heart rejoice, and my tongue was glad; moreover,also my flesh shall rest in hope, because Thou wilt not leave my soul in hades, neither wilt Thou suffer thine Holy one to see cor-

50

ruption. Thou hast made known to me the ways of life. Thou shalt
make me full of joy with Thy countenance. "Men and brethren,"
said Peter, in his successful sermon on the Day of Pentecost, "Let me
freely speak unto you of the Patriarch David, that he is both dead
and buried, and his sepulchre is with us unto this day, therefore being a Prophet and knowing that God had sworn with an oath to him,
that of the fruit of his loins, according to the flesh, he would raise up
Christ to sit upon His Throne; he seeing this before spake of the resurrection of Christ, that his soul was not left in hades neither did his
flesh see corruption," "whereof we are the witnesses."

The Apostle's reasoning was certainly understood by many of the
Jews, for "Three thousand of them were added that day to the
church. They all acknowledged David to be a Prophet—they all
knew that he had written, "The Lord said unto my Lord, sit thou on
my right hand till I make thy foes thy footstool." That the words
could not be applied to David is evident, for "he saw corruption," but
Christ did not; who, according to Moses, the Prophets and the Psalmist it behoved to suffer, to die, to be buried and to rise again from the
dead. "He will" said Isaiah, "swallow up death in victory," and
Hosea, prophesying of Him says, "Oh! death, I will be thy plagues.
Oh! grave, I will be thy destruction."*

---

*I have copied the above verbatim from the original manuscript of M. J. R. No
date nor name of any place is given in the sermon.   The Author.

Appeals In Behalf of Liberty.

CHAPTER VII.

To the Legislators of America:—

Citizens:—You stand in the place of God, to make laws for man. Justice and mercy should be stamped on all your proceedings. You are not ignorant of the principles of good government; you well know that to be the best government in which all the inherent rights of human nature are inviolably secured, legal authority is maintained and restricted to its objects, the power of the state is employed to promote the general happiness, and inequality itself tends to preserve equality of law and parity of obligation among all the members of the community. Legislators of the United States! are you ignorant of the signs of the times? You cannot be. The proximity of the West India Islands and the state of the Negroes, under the French Government, cannot escape your notice. But we have peace at home. Yes, sirs! Where is the man barbarous and stupid enough to give the name of peace to the silence, the force silence of slavery? It is indeed peace, but it is the peace of the tomb—the silence of slaves is terrible. It is the silence before a hurricane: the winds are yet hushed, but from the dark bosom of an immovable cloud darts the thunder, the signal of the tempest, which strikes at the moment the flash appears. The silence, that silence that force compels, is the principal cause of the miseries of nations, and of the destruction of their oppressors. Absolute authority was never designed for mortals—the best natures will abuse it. "It fills the mind of man with great and unreasonable conceits of himself, raises him to a belief that he is a superior species to the rest of mankind; so great is the danger, that when a man can do what he will, he will do what he can."

Slavery is productive of pride, luxury and licentiousness; and the dissoluteness of manners, which the unrestrained power of gratification produces in the slave-holder and managers, cannot fail sooner or later to involve in ruin the country where this abuse of reason and humanity is permitted. Legislators! will you wait until the cloud bursts on your heads? May the manes of a Franklin with his electrical rod prevent the shock! May the memory of those men who were martyrs to the cause of liberty inspire your souls to acts of righteousness and deeds of mercy! Proclaim the jubilee—you have no time to lose. If you are not expeditious the laurel will be taken from you and repentance will come too late. Shew yourselves therefore to be men who have the interest of your country at heart. And the philosopher shall not complain that "the rulers of America are not worthy to be trusted with an Empire, the most extensive that ever obtained a name, in any age or quarter of the globe."

I Am, Citizens,

Georgia, Feb., 1795.   PHILANTHROPOS.

————:o:————

TO THE MINISTERS OF RELIGION IN THE UNITED STATES OF AMERICA:—

MEN AND BRETHREN:—Your profession is honorable. You are in a situation to be useful. It is true, in several of the States a most mean, inconsistent and contemptible law deprives you of the common privilege of citizens I hope it will create in your souls a perfect hatred of tyranny in whatever shape it may form itself; that it will inspire your souls with fresh vigor in defending the glorious cause of liberty ; that it will cement together in one evangelical fraternity all the sects and parties among you—then you will have no enemy but vice, no friend but truth Love to God and man are the hinges upon which every door in your temples and habitations should turn. No spot on the habitable globe affords you greater scope to exercise and encourage philanthropy than America. Thousands of distressed Negroes in the bowels of your country groan for liberty at the altar of the unknown God. The Indians in a great measure surround your territories and wait for your mission· aries to tell them, "And the days of this ignorance God winked at" or passed by, 'but now commandeth all men everywhere to repent." O· sirs, remember that Indians and Negroes will rise up in judgment against you, if you do not exert your influence to emancipate the one and send messengers of peace to the other. Excuse not yourselves by saying "We have no influence, the people will not hear us." If the people will not hear your reasoning, follow them with your remonstrances. If they shun your places of worship, go to the streets, highways and hedges. Assure them that the Judge is at the door, that the day of retribution is at hand. Thus you will save your own souls and such as will receive your doctrine.

————:o:————

A FRAGMENT.

"And finally, to impart all the blessings we possess, or ask for ourselves, to the whole family of mankind."

Nobly said. Whilst anticipating the happy period when the application should be made even to Africans, I thought myself immediately transported to Mount Vernon, and there beheld the Defender of His Country, in conformity to his prayer, convening his Negroes together and addressing them thus:—"Brethren, you have long been my bondsmen; I have kept you as slaves, contrary to the laws of God and the natural rights of man—but as it has pleased the Almighty to open my eyes and inclined my heart to pray 'that the blessings we possess as white men may be imparted to the whole family of mankind,' I immediately set you at liberty, not doubting but all the inhabitants of the United States will follow my example in so equitable a deed. I call you my black children; I gave orders that you might be always used well, but I had no right to keep you slaves—you are such no longer. The day of your emancipation is the happiest of my life. It is the day wherein I have obtained the greatest conquest; I rejoice in it more than all my victories over the British Armies. My black brethren be free. You who are old and infirm I shall comfortably support for your past labors. Your children shall be instructed, and none of you in any way shall go away without ample satisfaction. Such of you as choose to remain with me shall be rewarded according to your merit and industry. Your offspring will soon become respectable citizens of America; but remember it must be by serving God and performing their duties towards men. Let me beseech you not to avenge your ancient wrongs. Look unto Christ and forgive your enemies. When I am no more in this world, think of George Washington."

With these words, I heard the united voices of the Negroes rending the air with exclamations of joy—"O no, Massa, we never forget you." The heavens smiled upon the deed, and I found myself back in Georgia.

PHILANTHROPOS

Fel ruary 25th, 1795.

AN ORATION

Delivered at

Greenville, Headquarters of the Western Army, North-West of the Ohio,

JULY 4th, 1795,

By the

REV. MORGAN J. RHEES,

A Late Emigrant From Wales.

———

PHILADELPHIA.
Printed by Lang & Ustick.
1795.

(From the Philadelphia Gazette.)

MR. BROWN:—

A copy of the enclosed oration, delivered on the late anniversary of American Independence, was presented to a citizen of Philadelphia. That citizen, wishing to make good use of it, forwards it to your press for publication—sensible that the perusal of it will afford pleasure to all the sincere lovers of Liberty! The Author is greatly and deservedly esteemed by all who know him.

Philadelphia, Sept. 7, 1795.   W. R.

An Oration.

CHAPTER VIII.

Illustrious Americans! Noble Patriots! You commemorate a glorious day—the Birthday of Freedom in the New World! Yes, Columbia, thou art free. The twentieth year of thy independence commences this day. Thou has taken the lead in regenerating the world. Look back, look forward; think of the past, anticipate the future and behold with astonishment the transactions of the present time! The globe revolves on the axis of Liberty; the new world has put the old in motion; the light of truth, running rapid like lightning, flashes convictions in the heart of every civilized nation. Yes, the thunder of American remonstrance has fallen so heavy on the head of the tyrant that other nations, encouraged by her example, will extirpate all despots from the earth.

O, France, although I do not justify thy excesses, I venerate thy magnanimity. If the sun of thy liberty has been eclipsed by a bloodthirsty Marat and a saturnine Robespiere, if their accomplices, the sons of faction, will darken thy horizon, the energy of the nation, the unparalleled success of thy armies, like a mighty rushing wind, will scatter the clouds and drive them from thy hemisphere. The sun of liberty will return with healing in its wings! Yes, its genial rays will restore the swooping spirit of the distressed, and give new energy to the champions of freedom Invincible Frenchmen, go on! Having laid your hands to the plough, look not back until the soil of Europe is made a proper fallow to receive the seeds of emancipation.

The popish beast has nearly numbered his days; the vassal kings, emperors and princes who have deluged the earth with blood, under their malign influence, shall soon take their exit with him to the same pit of destruction. Nor shall those potentates who have thrown off his yoke to ape his authority escape the punishment due for their crimes. They have, under the mask of mammonism, riveted the chains of slavery two-fold faster than Charlemagne had it in their power However, when the sons of Liberty will make a strong pull, a long pull and a pull all together, the brass bars, the iron gates, the gold and silver chains of despotism must be broken. Combined Sons of Freedom! go on until every bastile on earth, with the infernal dungeons of the ocean,* are destroyed like the Parisian prison.

Batavians and Belgians! rally to the standard of your deliverers, assist them to carry their conquests to the citadel of Rome that the tree of liberty may be p'anted once more on the banks of the Tiber. If the Court of Byzantium should be inimical to your progress, tell the monster Mahomed that the flag of freedom shall soon fly on the ramparts of Constantinople.

Neither the Ottoman Porte nor the infamous Catharine can long withstand the energy of freemen. Let them meet the haughty tyrant of the north in the fertile fields of Poland, and the vassals of that unhappy country shall be restored to liberty and equality. The Greeks and the Romans will then know that the fire of freedom is not extinguished.

Whilst I behold it kindling in every quarter of the globe, where shall I turn my eyes first? O, My Country!† My Country! My heart bleeds, my eyes become a fountain of waters when I think of thy fate—Ichabod may be written upon all thy borders, for the glory is departed! How is thy bright gold become dim? How are the sons of Liberty, the pearls of the nations cast into prisons and banished o'er the seas? O, my countrymen! my countrymen! how long will you be duped by a dogmatic administration which seems determined to destroy not only their own nation, but to mark their footsteps with devastation and blood wherever they go.

Infatuated Britons! I feel for your insanity, although four thousand miles from your coasts. Twenty years have elapsed since your American brethren have given you a practical example to resist despotism. Have they not emphatically told you that no government has a right to taxation without a free and equal representation?

Ancient Britons!‡ awake out of your sleep! Open your eyes! Why are your tyrants great? Because you kneel down and cringe to them. Rise up—you are their equals! If you cannot rise, creep to the ocean and the friendly waves will waft you over the Atlantic to the hospitable shores of America. If you cannot attain liberty in your own native country, "where liberty dwells, call that your country." Embark then for the Western World, which wants nothing but millions of good citizens, to make up the glory of all the earth. Quit the little despotic island which gave you birth, and leave the tyrants and slaves of your country to live and die together.

*The British Men-of-War.
†Great Britain.
‡The Welsh people.

Citizens of the United States: Be not frightened in beholding so many emigrants flocking to your territory. If all the inhabitants of the world were to pay you a visit, you can compliment each of them with half an acre of land.* But, sirs, look forward and behold with transports of joy this vast continent from the Gulf of St. Lawrence to the Gulf of Mexico, from the Pacific to the Atlantic, forming one grand Republic of Brethren.

At present it is impossible to calculate on the rapidity of revolutions. What formerly took a century to accomplish is brought to pass in a day. If the snow ball as it rolls, multiplies its magnitude, the torrent being checked for a season, runs with greater rapidity. So the cause of truth and liberty, being opposed by despots, will gain greater energy, and will eventually, like a mighty deluge, sweep every refuge of his from the earth. The little stone which Nebuchadnezzar saw, smote the image on its feet, ground it to powder, became a great mountain and filled the whole earth. So be it speedily. May the perfect law of liberty sway its sceptre of love, from the rising to the setting sun, from the centre of the globe to the extremities of the poles.

Citizens of United States: Whilst you commemorate a glorious resolution, call to mind your first principles of action—never forget them nor those who assisted you to put your principles in practice. May the curse of Meroz (Judges V) never fall upon America for not joining the heralds of freedom, whilst combatting the tyrants of Europe.

Citizens of America: Guard with jealousy the temple of Liberty. Protect her altars from being polluted with the offerings of force of fraud.

Citizens and Soldiers of America—Sons of Liberty: It is you I address. Banish from your land the remains of slavery. Be consistent with your congressional declaration of rights and you will be happy. Remember there never was nor will be a period when justice should not be do ic. Do what is just and leave the event with God. Justice is the pillar that upholds the whole fabric of human society, and mercy is the genial ray which cheers and warms the habitations of man. The perfection of our social character consists in properly tempering the two with one another. In holding that middle course which admits of our being just without being rigid and allows us to be generous without being unjust. May all the citizens of America be found in the performance of such social virtues as will secure them peace and happiness in this world and in the world to come, life everlasting, through Jesus Christ our Lord.

---

* (i. e). Within the limits of the United States—Indian Territory included.

HISTORY

OF THE

CITY OF BEULÁH;

ALSO OF

BEULAH BAPTIST CHURCH,

BY J F. BARNES,

CHAPTER IX.

In a valley on the head waters of the south fork of Black Lick Creek, in the midst of the Allegheny Mountains, about three miles west of Ebensburg, Cambria County, Pennsylvania, a few heaps of stones, covered with moss, trees and ferns, and here and there an excavation, nearly filled with debris and vegetation, mark the site of the extinct town of Beulah; whilst a grave-yard, located on an adjoining plateau, where numerous narrow mounds, with here and there moss-covered head and foot stones scarcely discernible for the vines and briars that cover this little cemetery, mark the last resting-place of many of the former citizens of this once thriving settlement.

We cannot conceive of a more complete and thorough abandonment and utter desolation than exist here at the present time, and yet this was once the scene of active, busy life. The inhabitants were full of energy, enthusiasm and enterprise, and they fondly cherished the expectation that Beulah would eventually become the centre of many thriving settlements.

At first glance, the visitor wonders why a colony should locate in such a desolate and secluded place. It seems to be isolated from the surrounding country. None of the principal thoroughfares pass through it. A township road, in miserable condition, scarcely wide enough for a vehicle to pass along, leads to and from the site of this

old town. But it was not always thus. In A. D. 1787, the Commonwealth of Pennsylvania being desirous of opening its territory lying
west of the Allegheny Mountains for settlement, surveyed and constructed a road from Frankstown, on the Juniata River, to East
Liberty, one of the suburbs of Pittsburg.

Frankstown, the eastern terminus of the this road, is probably
the oldest town in the Juniata Valley. Conrad Wiester mentions it in
his diary as early as 1748, and it is spoken of by traders who where
there in 1749 and 1750. It occupies the site of an old Indian settlement
called Assunepachla, which signifies a meeting of many waters, an
appropriate name, since in this vicinity four streams unite to form
the Frankstown branch of the Juniata River.

This road was known to the early settlers along the route as the
Frankstown Road, and even at the present time in that portion of
Pittsburgh formerly known as East Liberty, one of its streets is still
called the Frankstown Road, thus indicating the place where this
once famous thoroughfare connected with the Cumberland or Southern Turnpike.

Soon after its construction, this road became the main thoroughfare between the central and northeastern part of Pennsylvania and
Pittsburgh and the West. At that time, no iron nor salt were
produced west of the Allegheny Mountains, and these important and
almost indispensable articles were transported, in wagons and on
pack-saddles, from the Juniata Valley, across the mountains along
this road. More than that, this road became the main route of travel
for emigrants from the State of Connecticut to their newly acquired
territory in the State of Ohio, now known as the "Western Reserve."

We, living in this age of railroad and steamboat transportation
and travel, can have but an imperfect conception of the vast number
of horses and vehicles necessary to conduct a traffic of this kind.
Illustrative of this, permit me to state that my grandfather, Joseph
Barnes, kept a hotel and ferry on the same Frankstown Road,
where it crossed the Conemaugh River, two miles below the present
site of Blairsville, and my father, Henry Barnes, frequently told me
that it was no unusual thing for one hundred teams to stop with
them on the same night. It may be asked how they accommodated
so many. The answer is that the horses were usually tied to the
wagons and fed out of boxes attached thereto, whilst a large proportion of the teamsters and emigrants slept in their covered wagons or
schooners, as they are now called in the far West.

The site of Beulah was located on this busy thoroughfare. In
1797, Rev. Morgan John Rhees, aided and encouraged by his warm
personal friend and admirer, the distinguished Dr. Benjamin, Rush of

Philadelphia, purchased a large tract of land in what was at that time the north-western part of Somerset County, Pa. Mr. Rhees called this tract of land Cambria, in honor of his native Wales. He also laid out a town upon a portion of this tract and called it Beulah. It is a Welsh word meaning "Land of Freedom," and, as we shall see hereafter, Mr. Rhees' experience in his native land had been such that he could fully appreciate the advantage of dwelling in a land worthy of the name of Beulah. Judging from the plot of the town, which may be found among the records of Somerset County, the founder of Beulah must have entertained glowing anticipations of the future greatness of the place. The plot of Beulah is an exact counterpart of the original plot of the city of Philadelphia, being four miles square, with streets intersecting each other at right angles. We therefore feel warranted in saying that Beulah was once as large as Philadelphia, but we would not attempt to prove that it was ever as densely populated. Dr. Cathcart, in the Baptist Encyclopedia, seems to convey the impression that Dr. Rush was a partner with Rev. Rhees in this enterprise; but we have examined some twenty-five or thirty original title papers, and in each and every instance Morgan J. Rhees was the only person mentioned in the body of the deed, as the owner and disposer of the lands, and his signature is the only one attached to those title papers. And just here I shall remark that the signature of Morgan J. Rhees was as bold, but more elegant, than that of John Hancock when he signed the Declaration of American Independence.

Beulah continued to flourish for some time after it was located. Mr. Rhees brought quite a number of Welsh families with him from Philadelphia, and others were attracted to the place in anticipation of the future greatness of the "Mountain City." Some sixty or seventy good, substantial log buildings were erected in the centre of the city, whilst numerous clearings were opened up and homes established in its suburbs; and for miles around, the country was known by the name of Beulah instead of Cambria, the name originally given by Mr. Rhees to that portion of his purchase lying outside of the city limits. This will explain what I meant when in a former article I stated that Thomas E. Thomas resided on a farm near Beulah, three miles west of Ebensburg. To be more explicit, I should have stated that the farm formerly occupied by Thomas E. Thomas is on the Ebensburg and Kittanning Turnpike, seven miles west of Ebensburg and four miles from the site of the Beulah Baptist meeting-house.

At one time, Beulah had a population of upwards of 300. There were located in the city two hotels, a store, one church, a mill, a school, and a library containing about 600 volumes, besides a sufficient number of mechanical shops to meet the requirements of the community and travelers. We examined a list of the books belonging to "The Cambrian Library at Beulah," and found the selection to have been a very good one. The Bible is the first named on the list. Then follows such books as Doddridge's Works, Hall's Contemplations, etc., etc. History, literature, the arts and sciences, mechanics and even military tactics are all represented on the list. We also find works in different languages named on the list, among which are Greek, Latin and French Testaments. A newspaper was published by Morgan J. Rhees at Beulah the press work being done in Philadelphia.

It was but natural that Morgan J. Rhees, having taken such a lively interest in the education of the young people in his native land, should establish a school in his own colony soon after its settlement. A Sabbath school was organized in 1797, and a day school was established soon afterwards. We presume that Bro. Rhees conducted his school at Beulah upon the same principle that he conducted his school in Wales, that is, by charging nothing for tuition, thus making them virtually free schools. However, in 1802, Rev. Henry George, a Baptist minister, having emigrated from Wales, and he having been obliged to leave his family in his native land for lack of funds to bring them with him, opened a subscription school at Beulah for the purpose of raising money to send for his family. This school was kept in the meeting-house, and some of the pupils came from a distance of five or six miles, following old Indian trails through dense forests. It was no unusual thing for the children to hear the howling of wolves, the growling of bears, and the shrieks of panthers as they journeyed homewatd in the evenings.

The Sabbath-school and day-school established by Bro. Rhees at Beulah were undoubtedly the first schools established within the limits of Cambria County, and the pay school, opened by Rev. Henry George at Beulah, was the second of that kind within that county, Prince Gallitzin having established a school for the education of his parishioners at Loretta in the spring of 1800, and employed a Mr. O'Connor to serve as teacher.

For more than half a century after all the other buildings at Beulah had disappeared, there remained a massive structure that excited the curiosity of every one who visited the place. Whilst all the other buildings had been constructed of hewn logs, erected upon solid foundations of stone, this building, measuring 28 feet by 32 feet, and being full two stories high, besides a cellar of unusual depth, was built of large blocks of rocks quarried in that vicinity. Some suppose it was built for a jail; others that it was intended for a court-house; others that it was for a library and town hall; but from the best information I could obtain, the building was a private enterprise, began by a man named Philips, who ran it up to the height of two full stories, but who, for some cause, abandoned it, never even putting a roof upon it.

My opinion is that, inasmuch as the citizens of Beulah entertained ardent expectations of their town becoming the county seat of the new county about to be formed of parts of Bedford, Huntingdon and Somerset Counties, this man Phillps, perhaps acting under the advice and direction of capitalists who were booming the town, built this structure in anticipation of its soon being required for county purposes, and that he abandoned it without completing it, when Ebensburg, instead of Beulah, was selected as the county seat of Cambria County. This structure was torn down some time ago, and the stones were hauled to Ebensburg, and used in building either the new court-house or jail at that place.

From an examination of the consideration received for lots sold in Beulah, as specefied in deeds dated in 1797, 1798 and 1799, we learn that lots located on Milk, Kid, Lamb and Third Streets usually sold for about $50 each, whilst lots sold on Joy, Hope and some other streets were sold at $10 each. As the deeds for these lots were all made by Morgan J. Rhees, to the parties who purchased them, we infer they were not improved lots, and since the payments are always required to be made in "lawful silver money of the United States" they certainly were sold at their full value, when we reflect upon the scarcity of money and its purchasing power at that time. In those days, 50 dollars would have purchased several hundred acres of unimproved land in almost any part of the territory now embraced within the limits of this Association.

Among those who purchased lots, we find the names of Thomas W. Jones, lot No. 10, East Lamb Street, price $50. Date of deed, Oct. 1, 1797. Rees Lloyd, lot No. 7, East Joy Street, price $10. Date of deed, Nov. 22, 1797. Ebenezer Hickling, lots Nos, 33, 34 and 39, East Milk Street, price $50 each. Date of deed, June 29, 1799 Also Deborah Taylor, lot No. 11, East Third Street, price $50. Date of deed, Oct. 12, 1799.

Beulah continued to flourish until A. D. 1805, when it was decided that of the three towns, Munster, Ebensburg and Beulah, aspiring to become the county seat of the new county, of Cambria, which had been formed during the previous year, the one should be selected that was located the nearest to the geographical center of the new county. A survey of the territory embraced within this county showed that Ebensburg was located exactly in the center, and it therefore became the county seat, notwithstanding that Beulah had many natural advantages not possessed by the former place. Instead of being located on top of a steep hill, it occupied a valley. A stream of water ran through the place, and numerous, cool, refreshing springs were in and around it, whilst the adjoining hills were full of coal and other minerals. The lowest depression of the Allegheny Mountains is on the head-waters of the stream that passes through Beulah, and it is probable that if there had been an important county town located at Beulah the Pennsylvania Canal and also the Pennsylvania Railroad would have followed that route. In that event, the county seat of Cambria County, instead of being a little country town, depending upon the practice in its courts for its main support, might possibly have become a large manufacturing city.

From the time that Ebensburg was selected as the county seat, Beulah began to decline. Its founder and most influential friend, Rev. Rhees, was dead. Many of its most active and energetic citizens removed from the place; and, if anything further was needed to annihilate it, that event soon occurred. Capitalists, seeing the immense amount of travel along the Frankstown Road, secured a charter and constructed the great "Northern Turnpike," extending from Huntingdon to Pittsburg. The easy grade and solid road-bed of this new thoroughfare diverted the travel from the Frankstown road, for, although toll-gates were numerous, the increase in the weight that could be hauled, and the increased distance that could be traveled, in a given length of time, on this new route, more than compensated for the additional expense in the way of tolls. Unfortunately for Beulah, this new road did not pass through it, leaving it about one mile to the north. However, there was still a little travel through that place to Indiana and adjacent towns, but even that was taken away by the construction of the "Clay Turnpike" from Ebensburg to Kittanning. This road left Beulah three miles to the south, thereby almost isolating it from communication with the commercial world.

Justice appears to have been meted out without fear or favor, and Sunday laws were not a dead letter on the statute books in those days. From records of proceedings in the Court of George Roberts, "Associate Judge in and for the County of Somerset," we discover that one man was fined four dollars "for carrying a large bag of oats, on a horse, through the streets on the Sabbath day, commonly called Sunday." And on a number of other occasions persons were fined four dollars for driving loaded teams and wagons on the Sabbath. Also the law against profanity appears to have been rigidly enforced. I thought to myself as I read the names of those who had been found guilty and fined in a Civil Court for taking the name of the Lord in vain, what a disgraceful record it was for them to leave behind them whilst their bodies lie mingling with the dust; but, oh! how dreadful it will be when they shall be arraigned before the high court of Heaven for the same offense, before the Great

Judge of the quick and the dead, who has said, "Thou shalt not take the name of the Lord thy God in vain, for the Lord will not hold him guiltless that taketh His name in vain."

The graves of a few of the early settlers, who were buried in the churchyard, are marked by grave stones; among whom are, Thomas W. Jones; who died March 14, 1808, aged 36 years. At the time of his death he held the offices of Justice of the Peace and Surveyor, having been appointed to those positions by the Governor of Pennsylvania. Elizabeth Jenkins died Sept. 20, 1828, aged 51 years; Ann Jones died Feb 2, 1832, aged 75 years; Elias Rowland died July 24, 1858, aged 93 years; Catharine, wife of Elias Rowland, died April 24, 1840, aged 67 years; William Roberts died Jan. 7, 1822, aged 51 years; and his wife, Elizabeth Roberts, died Sept. 24, 1850, aged 76 years; William Davis died March 7, 1826, aged 63 years.

Before closing this notice of the settlement, decadence and abandonment of Beulah, I shall quote from a letter, written many years ago by Judge George Roberts, who afterwards became pastor of the Congregational Church at Ebensburg He says: "In the years 1794, 1795 and 1796 quite a number of Welsh families emigrated to America for the purpose of establishing a colony in some suitable and convenient place. Mr. Rhees, who acted as their leader, petitioned Congress to grant them a piece of land for that purpose. In this he did not succeed, and other petitions were equally unsuccessful. It seemed as if Providence closed every door against them, except the one on top of the Allegheny Mountains. Mr. Rhees formed a church of forty or fifty Welsh people, who found a home in Philadelphia. This church was composed of an equal number of Congregationalists, Calvinistic-Methodists and Baptists."

From what we can learn, Rev. Rees Lloyd, a Congregational minister who had recently emigrated from Wales, appears to have been a co-laborer with Bro. Rhees in supplying the spiritual wants of this congregation, although he did not come with Bro. Rhees to Beulah, he having taken a number of Welsh people with him and established a colony in the winter of 1796-7, where Ebensburg was afterwards located. From the statements made by Judge Roberts, it might be inferred that Congress gave the land to the colonists at Beulah; but from abundant data in our possessions, we are satisfied that Mr. Rhees, assisted by his friends, purchased the territory. But even if we had no other evidence at hand, the fact that this land belonged, at that time, to the State of Pennsylvania would be sufficient to prove that the land could not have been given to Rhees and his friends by Congress.

Having given more space to a history of Beulah than I intended doing, I shall now attempt to trace the history of the Baptist Church located there.

I found it a difficult matter to secure accurate information respecting this ancient church. Almost one hundred years have passed away since its organization, and unfortunately the Minute Book and Church Records have been lost. Rev. David Jenkins, who was, at one time, pastor of the Welsh Baptist Church at Ebensburg, borrowed the Minute Book of that church, which also contained the records of Beulah Church, and took it with him to the State of New York. He afterwards removed to Ohio, where he died, and all traces of this book of records have been lost.

Some diversity of opinion exists as to the date of the organization of Beulah Church. Benedict says: "At Beulah, in the midst of the Alleghany Mountains, a church was founded by emigrants from Wales in 1797, under the direction of Morgan J. Rhees."

Again, a Welsh historical magazine, called the "Star of Gomer," says: "In 1797 a Baptist church was founded at Beulah upon the principle of close communion, and the following Articles were adopted as the Religious Constitution of the new settlement :"

Article I.—This Union shall be called the Christian Church.

Article II.—It must never be called by any other name, nor controlled by any particular opinions of any man, or party of men.

Article III.—Jesus Christ is the only head, believers the only members, and the New Testament the only rule of brotherhood.

Article IV.—In intellectual things, every member shall enjoy his own opinions, and converse freely upon any subject; but in discipline, minute conformity with the commands of Christ is required.

Article V.—Every separate society that shall unite with this Association, shall have power to receive their members, elect their officers and, in case of misconduct, to discipline them.

Article VI.—The representatives of the various congregations shall meet from time to time, at an appointed place, for consultation in relation to the advancement and prosperity of the whole cause.

Article VII.—In every meeting for religious worship, collections shall be made to support the poor and spread the gospel in the midst of the pagans.

These Articles of Confederation read more like those usually adopted by a community rather than Articles adopted for the formation of a church, and yet, when compared with the Articles presented by that great apostle of religious liberty, Roger Williams, for the organization of his church and settlement in Rhode Island, we discover that there is, to say the least of it, a similarity between them.

From an examination of Articles 5 and 6, we discover that these pioneers, who organized Beulah Church, entertained glowing anticipations respecting the future greatness and influence of their organization. They seemed to cherish the idea that the time would eventually come when Beulah Church would be the centre around which would cluster many similar societies, and, as we shall learn hereafter, they made an earnest effort to make it such by sending out missionaries to preach the Gospel in nearly all parts of our State. The Lord manifoldly blessed the labors of these missionaries, resulting in the ingathering of many souls into the fold of Christ; but the ambitious desires of Beulah Church were never realized.

The first pastor of Beulah Church was Morgan J. Rhys. He was nominally their pastor for about four years; but duties of another description required him to be absent a considerable portion of the time. At his suggestion the church extended a call to Richard Michaels, of Anglesea, Wales. He reached Beulah sometime in 1801, and assumed the pastorate of Beulah Church; but he was only permitted to spend one Lord's Day with his people. He only lived seven days after his arrival at Beulah.

The next pastor was Joseph Powell, of Tonoloway; but as he was an old man and had a great distance to travel to reach Beulah Church, he soon resigned.

He was succeeded by Timothy Davies, who appears to have been their pastor from the time of the resignation of Bro. Powell until about A. D. 1813. At all events, we can gain no information as there having been any other pastor elected until that time; but there being quite a number of ordained ministers holding fellowship with that church, the pulpit was frequently occupied by home talent. The church was greatly blessed, and her numbers and efficiency very much enlarged, during the pastorate of Timothy Davies.

In 1813, William Williams was elected pastor, and in 1815, many of the young people having become Anglicized, and also persons who were not familiar with the Welsh language having moved into the community, Thomas Williams, an Englishman, who had recently been ordained at Beulah, was elected co-pastor with William Williams, the latter continuing to preach in Welsh while the former preached in English. This relation or co-partnership continued until 1829, when William Williams resigned. Thomas Williams continued to serve as pastor until 1834, when he also resigned to engage in mission work in the western part of the State under the auspices of the State Convention—a work for which he was especially qualified, having spent a large proportion of the time while he was pastor of the Beulah Church in visiting destitute parts of this State.

He was succeded by Benjamin Davies, a nephew and foster son of Timothy Davies, a former pastor of Beulah Church. During the pastorate of Benjamin Davies, they built a meeting-house in Ebensburg, and removed there; but they still retained the name of Beulah

Baptist Church. We have no evidence that they at any time, abandoned the work at Beulah, inasmuch as quite a large number of their most efficient members continued to reside at or near that place for many years afterward, and about this time, in their letter to Centre Association, they speak of having two meeting-houses. They also continued regular ministrations of the Word and ordinances at an out-station they had established in 1838 on the Ebensburg and Kittaning Turnpike, six miles west of the former place. After passing through various trials and vicissitudes, this society was, in 1859, permanently organized as the Bethel Baptist Church, whose fellowship and hospitality we are permitted to enjoy during the present anniversary of Indiana Association.

It was during the pastorate of Benjamin Davies that an event occurred which, if there were tears in Heaven, the bright angels and redeemed ones would have gazed upon in astonishment and wept over the scene. The pernicious teachings of Alexander Campbell had been infused into the minds of a large proportion of the members of Beulah Baptist Church. Heretofore, all had been peace and harmony. Their hearts were united by the ties of Christian fellowship and love. They shared each other's burdens and woes, and whatever contributed to the happiness of one increased the joys of all.

> How pleasant thus to dwell below
> In fellowship and love.

But now, Oh, how changed! Angry controversy took the place of brotherly greeting, and hot discussions on Baptismal Regeneration. Salvation by Works and not by Faith, "The power and influence of the Holy Spirit exists in the Bible and does not act directly upon the heart of the sinner." The discussion of these and many other schismatical theories was substituted for prayerful endeavors to promote God's glory in the salvation of souls. These doctrines and theories are not new, similar errors having crept into and disruptured many churches during the early centuries of the Christian era.

There is a species of formalism connected with the theory and practice of the teachings of Alexander Campbell that render them very acceptable to the carnal mind, because they open up an easy road to salvation, when compared with the road traveled over, and described by that old fogy Baptist preacher, John Bunyan, who preferred to remain in Bedford jail as a prisoner rather than purchase his freedom by selling the truth.

Among those who became infected with these heterodoxical views was Benjamin Davies, who was at that time pastor of Beulah Church, and he taught these views from the pulpit. When remonstrated with by the ministers who had grown gray in the services of the Master. he, like weak, poor, deluded, self-willed Rehoboam, refused to hearken to the counsel of the old men.

This spirit of contentiou and strife continued for a year or more, when, finding that the two factions could not do efficient work so long as they were nominally one organization, they, in 1836, by mutual consent, called an advisory council This council was presided over by Rev. George I. Miles. After hearing statements from each of the contending factions, and finding it imposssible to effect a reconciliation between them, the council recommended that all those in favor of organizing a Campbellite Church should manifest their desire by going to and standing up at one side of the meeting-house, while those who were in favor of adhering to the old faith and Baptist principles should occupy a similar position on the opposite side of the house.

Some of the members of each faction were very prompt in assuming their respective places and positions, whilst others hesitated about going to either side of the house. The Baptists made no efforts to persuade any one to come with them. whilst a number of the Campbellites, among whom were Benjamin Davies, Festus Tibbett and John Lloyd, Postmaster at Ebensburg, were very active in their efforts to persuade others to come to their side of the house.

After all the members of Beulah Church, who were present on that occasion, had taken their places, it was discovered that there were just fifty persons on each side of the house. There they stool, gazing into each other's faces, those who for many long years had felt the full force of the poet's sentiment expressed in the couplet,

> Blest be the tie that binds
> Our hearts in Christian love.

How often had their hearts thrilled with joy as they grasped each other's hands and thought of this tie that bound them to Christ and to each other; but now that tie was broken, and an impassable gulf lay between them.

Oh, what a mournful scene! And, Oh! what a contrast between those occupying the different sides of the house. At the head of the column on one side of the house was seen the gray heads and bent forms of William Williams and Thomas Williams, both of whom had for many years served as pastors of Beulah Church, and both of whom had spent the best days of their lives in an earnest effort to persude others to accept the truth in the love of the truth. Beside them, stood their aged companions, and many others who had grown gray in the Master's service. Sorrow and sadness were depicted upon their countenances, and tears trickled down their cheeks as they thought of the disruption of the church they loved so well, and of the alienation of Christian friends so dear to them.

At the head of the column on the opposite side of the house, stood a younger class, such men as Benjamin Davies, Festus Tibbett and John Lloyd. A triumphant and defiant look was manifestly expressed upon their countenances. They felt no sorrow for the disruption of the church. In fact, that was but a consummation of their desires, and a realization of what they had been working for. Their effort had all along been to make proselytes from the Baptist church, instead of going out into the world to seek and to save the lost and erring ones. In doing this, they were but following the usual pratice and policy of Campbellites in general.

Proselyting is their main forte, and I have often thought that the words of the blessed Lord, recorded in the fifteenth verse of the twenty-third chapter of Matthew, would apply with as much force to the Campbellites as they did to the persons to whom they were addressed nearly 1900 years ago. "Woe unto you, scribes and Pharisees, hypocrites! for ye compass sea and land to make one proselyte; and when he is made, ye make him two-fold more the child of hell than yourselves."

For some time after the separation, both organizations continued to worship in the same house, occupying it at different hours of the same day. Notwithstanding this precaution, the members of the two different organizations would frequently meet at the house of worship, and angry and unprofitable discussions would arise. The Baptists growing weary of this style of pugilistic Christianity proposed to sell their interest in the church property for whatever they could get for it. The Campbellites offered them $128 for their interest, and they accepted it. The Baptists then built a small meeting-house on one of the back streets in Ebensburg, where they could worship God in peace. They subsequently erected a more commodious house in a more central locality of the same town.

David Williams, son of Thomas Williams, a former pastor of Beulah Church, appears to have served as pastor of this church for sometime after the separation, and we observe that in 1840, Beulah Church, David Williams, pastor, with 77 members, received a letter of dismissal and recommendation from Centre Association to unite with the Welsh Association of Pittsburg.

Shortly afterwards, another separation took place in Beulah Church. Prior to this time, Beulah had been a member of Associations using the English language; but now, since their union with the Welsh Association, all the Minutes of Associational Anniversaries, and other documents, were printed in the Welsh language. This was very unsatisfactory to the English-speaking portion of the membership. The young people in particular were losing an interest in the meetings, and some of them were wandering away and uniting with churches of other denominations. In order to retain this portion of their membership, it was deemed best that they should form two separate and distinct organizations. They were therefore divided into what was known as the Welsh and the English churches. The Welsh Church retained the name of Beulah and the English adopted the name of the Ebensburg Baptist Church. This separation was effected on the most amicable terms, everyone believing it to be for the best. The Welsh Church retained the meeting-house, but they assisted the English Church in erecting a house of worship.

Richard Roberts, who was pastor of Beulah Church at the time the two branches were formed, continued to serve as pastor of the Welsh Church until his death, he having been killed by the limb of a tree falling upon him. He was succeeded by David Jenkins, followed by Evan Thomas and others.

Thomas Williams, Thomas E. Thomas and Samuel Furman were successively pastors of the English or Ebensburg Church. The members of this church were very poor in this world's goods; but the Lord poured out spiritual blessings upon them so long as they continued faithful to the cause under which they had enlisted. Unfortunately, the attention of some of the brethren became engrossed with the spirit manifested and principles taught by the churches of the now extinct Conemaugh Association, an organization mainly built upon the platform of "No fellowship with slave-holders," and as others of the membership differed with them in regard to this matter it created dissensions that deprived the church of its influence and usefulness. This left the church in a languishing condition, and had it not been for the vitality that existed in an out-station, where they had built a meeting-house, called the North Church, now known as Bethesda, the probability is that the Ebensburg Church would have become extinct.

Early in its history Beulah Church united with the Redstone Baptist Association, whose territory lay in the southwestern part of Pennsylvania, the same territory that is at present occupied by Monongahela, Ten Mile, Pan handle and Pittsburg Associations.

In 1824, Beulah withdrew from Redstone Association, and united with the Juniata Baptist Association because the latter was more accessible. It at that time reported 96 members, Thomas Williams and William Williams, joint pastors. Among the delegates from Beulah to that anniversary was Thomas E. Thomas, licentiate. However, he was ordained at Beulah sometime during the same year.

At the next session, held with the Mill Creek Church, Beulah was honored by one of their pastors, Thomas Williams, being elected Moderator of Juniata Association.

On the 15th, 16th and 17th days of October, 1829, Juniata Association held its annual anniversary with the Beulah Baptist Church at Beula. Among the visitors present on that occasion was Rev. John Thomas, half brother of Dr. Shadrach, representing Redstone Association. Rev. William Shadrach, who was then quite a young man, and who had been ordained at Mt. Pleasant during the previous year, was there also, and he preached before the Association on Friday, October 16th, from Col. i. 28. And doubtless the mother of these two boys, Mrs. Mary Shadrach, was there also for before the organization of Two Lick Baptist Church, she was a member of and a frequent worshipper at Beulah Church. I imagine that her heart would be filled with a mother's pride and emotion when she saw her "Will Bach," or dear little Willie, as she affectionately called him, thus honored by being so prominently brought before such an august assembly.

Beulah Church was a member of Juniata Association for a period of ten years, and during that time it reported Thomas Williams and William Williams as joint pastors, and it also reported eight others, namely, William Tibbett, Benjamin Tibbett, Benjamin Davies, Festus Tibbett, John J. Evans, John Jones, William Roberts and Thomas E. Thomas as ordained ministers holding their fellowship in that church.

In 1834, Beulah Church, with 51 members, withdrew from the Juniata Association and united with the Centre Association, that being the fourth anniversary of that body.

In tracing the history of Beulah Church, we find that from its very organization it was emphatically a missionary church, and as such in strong contrast with many of the churches with which it affiliated whilst it was a member of Redstone and Juniata Associations.

To be ordained at Beulah Church meant go out into the world and preach the gospel in destitute places. The sons of Beulah visited nearly all parts of our beloved State, preaching the gospel and baptizing thousands of believers into fellowship with Christ Jesus. What if even the site of Beulah City and Beulah Church be scarcely known, yet they accomplished a grand and noble work in their day and generation, laying broad and deep the foundations of numerous flourishing and permanently established churches, occupying territory as far west as Pittsburg, and as far east as the central counties on the Maryland border line.

In the territory, at present embraced within the limits of Indiana Association, they laid the foundation and organized Two Lick Baptist Church, and assisted in building up her outstations, some of which subsequently became and are at the present time flourishing church organizations. They also extended their missionary work along the Chestnut Ridge and Laurel Hill in Indiana County, and they established a church called the Black Lick Baptist Church, among the Stephenses and Barcklays, near the present site of Dilltown. That church was subsequently removed to Mechanicsburg, Indiana County, taking the name of the Brush Valley Baptist Church. However, Baptist sentiment permeates the whole neighborhood, where this church was originally located, and it is, therefore, a promising field for missionary labor, and as such it should be cultivated by our own Association.

In speaking of this Black Lick Church, we must not get confused by supposing it to be the same church that is at present known by that name. The present Black Lick Church was organized in 1861, and it is located at a point at least 25 miles distant from the place where the original Black Lick Church was established, and it never had any connection with the original church of that name.

In those early days, the compensation awarded to a pastor was exceedingly small, and a member of a church who contributed one or two dollars towards the pastor's salary was regarded as being unnecessarily extravagant in that direction. The labor of those early pioneer preachers was, to a great extent, a labor of love, and they, like the great apostle to the Gentiles, depended upon the labor of their hands for their main support.

But this willingness to sacrifice ease and comfort for the sake of enjoying religious privileges was not confined to the preachers alone. The people were in earnest in their profession of religion in those days and they did not hesitate to undertake what would be regarded as herculean, if not impossible, tasks, by people of the present generation, in order to enjoy their privileges and discharge their duties as Christians. Where could we find sisters now-a-days who would be willing to attempt to do as Mary Shadrach very often did, walk from Two Lick to Beulah, over rough roads, a distance of nearly twenty-five miles, in order that she might enjoy the privileges of the sanctuary. Another of these earnest, self-sacrificing sisters was "Old Kitty Rees," as she was familiarly called, who used to walk from the "Broad Fording," where Coheville is now located, to Beulah, a distance of over 36 miles, and she was always present on every communion occasion.

Family Records.

CHAPTER X.
Rhees Family.

I.   John Rhys, of Graddfa, Llanfabon, Glamorganshire, Wales, had a son named Morgan John Rhys.

II.   Rev. Morgan John (Rees) Rhees, married Ann Loxley; had son

II.   1. John Loxley Rhees, married Rebecca McElwee; had
IV.   a. Rebecca Ann Rhees, died unmarried.
IV.   b. Catharine Loxley Rhees, living unmarried.
IV.   c. Lily Rhees, died unmarried.
IV.   d. Ellen Duval Rhees, died unmarried.
IV.   e. Dr. Morgan John Rhees, married Charlotte L. Head
IV.   f. Rev. Henry Holcombe Rhees, married Hetty Parsons.
IV.   g. Alice Bunting Rhees, married Edw. Parsons.

II.   2. Dr. Benjamin Rush Rhees, married Margaret Grace Rhees; had
IV.   h. Henry Shippen Rhees, died unmarried.
IV.   i. Ann Loxley Rhees, died unmarried.
IV.   j. William Jones Rhees, married Laura O. Clarke
          "   "   "   "   Romenia F. Ellis.

II.   3. Mary Rhees, married Rev. Timothy Jackson; had
IV.   k. Anna Rhees Jackson, married Chas. W. Atkinson.
          "   "   "   "   Benj. A. Stevens.
IV.   l. Martha Jackson, married J. V. W. Montague.
IV.   m. Col. James Jackson, married Ida Beach.
          "   "   "   "   Ella Green.
IV.   n. Jane Jackson, married Irving Card.

II.   4. Morgan John Rhees, married Grace Wallis Evans; had
IV.   o. Benj. Rush Rhees, died unmarried.
IV.   p. John Evans Rhees, married Anne H. McCutchen
IV.   q. Mary Erwin Rhees, married Chas. G. Hammond.

IV	r.	Annie E. Rhees, married Isaac H Seelye.
III.	5.	Eliza Rhees, married Rev. Nicholas Murray; had
IV.	s.	Elizabeth C. Murray, died unmarried.
IV.	t	John M. Murray, died unmarried.
IV.	u.	Wm W. Murray, died unmarried.
IV.	v.	Ann Rhees Murray, died unmarried.
IV.	w.	Mary Jones Murray, married Henry L. Butler.
IV.	x.	Rosa Murray, living unmarried.
IV.	y.	Nicholas Murray, living unmarried
IV.	z.	Margaret Murray, died unmarried.
IV.	2a.	Catharine L. Murray. died unmarried.
IV.	2b.	Thos. C. Murray, died unmarried.
IV.	e.	Dr. Morgan John Rhees and Charlotte Head had
V	a.	Morgan J. Rhees, living unmarried.
V.	b.	Joseph L. Rhees, living unmarried
IV.	f.	Rev. Henry H. Rhees and Hetty Parsons had no children.
IV.	g.	Alice B. Rhees and Edward Parsons had
V.	c.	Prof. Frank Parsons, living unmarried.
V.	d.	Hattie R. Parsons, married James F. Griffin.
V.	e.	Loxley R. Parsons, living unmarried.
IV.	j.	Wm. Jones Rhees and Laura O Clarke (1st wife) had
V.	f.	Frances A. Rhees, married Jos. U. Burket.
IV.	j.	Wm. Jones Rhees and Romenia F. Ellis (2d wife) had
V.	g.	William Henry Rhees, living unmarried.
V.	h.	Charles F. Rhees, died unmarried.
V.	i.	Grace M. Rhees. living unmarried.
V.	j.	Flora G. Rhees, living unmarried.
V.	k.	Benj. Rush Rhees, living unmarried.
IV.	k.	Anna Rhees Jackson and Chas. W. Atkinson had
V.	l.	Mabel Atkinson, living unmarried.
V.	m.	Anna M Atkinson, died unmarried.
V.	n.	Joseph H. Atkinson, living unmarried.
V.	o.	Lizzie M. Atkinson, married.
IV.	l.	Martha Jackson and J. V. W. Montague had
V.	p.	Mary L. Montague, living unmarried.
V.	q.	Richard W. Montague, married Ellen A. Burton.
V.	r.	Carrie R. Montague, living unmarried.
V.	s.	Jennie E. Montague, married Roswell S. Lamson.
V.	t.	James J. Montague, living unmarried.
IV.	m.	Col. James Jackson and Ida Beach had

V.   u. Rhees Jackson, living, unmarried.
V.   v   Marion B. Jackson, living, unmarried.
IV.   p. John Evans Rhees and Anne H. McCutchen had
V.   y. Lillie G. Rhees, married Edw. St. John.
V.   w. Rev. Rush Rhees ✗
V.   x. Carrie Rhees, died, unmarried
IV.   q. Mary Erwin Rhees and Chas. G. Hammond had
V.   z   Annie R. Hammond, married Chas. H. Warren.
V.   aa. Mary G. Hammond, died, unmarried.
IV.   s   Annie E. Rhees and Isaac H. Seelye had
V.   bb. Carrie M. Seelye, died, unmarried
V.   cc. Frank R. Seelye, married Florence V. Hess.
IV.   w. Mary Jones Murray. married Henry L. Butler; had
V.   dd. Nicholas Murray Butler, married Susanna F
              Schuyler.
V.   ee. Henry M. Butler, married Carrie Kenny.
V.   ff. Wm. C. Butler, married Eleanor E. Hughes.

V.   d   Hettie R. Parsons and James F. Griffin had
VI.   a. James B. Griffin, living, unmarried.
VI.   b. John A. Griffin, living, unmarried
VI.   c. Frank L. Griffin, living, unmarried.

V.   f. Frances A. Rhees and Joseph U. Burket had
VI   d. Frances Burket, living, unmarried.

V.   y. Lillie G Rhees and Edward St. John had
VI.   e. Morgan Rhees St. John, living, unmarried.
VI.   f. Ancel St John, living, unmarried.
VI.   g   Grace E St. John, living, unmarried.

V.   bb. Frank Rhees Seelye and Florence V. Hess had
VI.   h. Grace H. Seelye, living, unmarried.
VI.   i. Merritt B. Seelye, living, unmarried.
VI.   j. Carrie H. Seelye, living, unmarried.

V.   dd. Nicholas Murray Butler and Susanna E. Schuyler had
VI.   k   Sarah S. Butler, living, unmarried.

V.   ee. Henry M. Butler and Carrie Kenny had
VI.   l. Mary M. Butler, living, unmarried.
VI.   m. Rosa M. Butler, living, unmarried.
VI.   n. Henry L. Butler, living, unmarried.

V.   ff. Wm. C. Butler and Eleanor E. Hughes had
VI.   o. Wm. C. Butler, living, unmarried.

Great—grandson — now (1901)

Loxley Family.

I. Benjamin Loxley, married Catharine Cox; had

   II. 1.   Elizabeth Loxley, died unmarried.
   II. 2.   Mary Loxley, died unmarried.
   II. 3.   Jane Loxley, married Samuel Clarke.
   II. 4.   John Loxley, died unmarried.
   II. 5.   Catherine Loxley, died unmarried.
   II. 6.   Stephen Loxley, died unmarried.
   II. 7.   Elizabeth Loxley, married Lloyd Jones.
   II. 8.   John Loxley, died unmarried.
   II. 9.   Catherine Loxley, married John Smith.
   II. 10.   Ann Loxley, married Rev. Morgan John Rhees.
   II. 11.   George Washington Loxley, married Ann Taylor.
   II. 12.   Catherine Loxley, died unmarried.

II. 3.   Jane Loxley, married Samuel Clarke; had

      Elizabeth B. Clarke, died unmarried.
      Catherine L. Clark, died unmarried,
      Mary J. Clarke, died unmarried.
      William Jones Clark, died unmarried.
      Robert J. Clarke, died unmarried.
      Israel L. Clarke, died unmarried.
      Eliza Clarke, died unmarried.
      Uselma A. Clarke, died unmarried.
      Marian Clarke, died unmarried.
      Lloyd M. Clarke, died unmarried.

II. 7.   Elizabeth Loxley, married Lloyd Jones; had

   III. 11.   Benjamin Loxley Jones, died unmarried.
   III. 12.   Eleanor Jones, married Edw. Duval.
   III. 13.   Susan F. Jones, died unmarried.
   III 14.   Henry Jones, died unmarried.
   III. 15.   Elizabeth B. Jones, died unmarried.
   III. 16.   Rebecca Ann Jones, died unmarried.
   III. 17.   Charlotte Jones, married Cyrus T. Smith.
   III. 18.   Catherine L. Jones, died unmarried.

II 9. Catherine Loxley married John Smith; had
    III. 19. Cyrus T. Smith married Charlotte Jones.
    III. 20. Benjamin L. Smith died unmarried.
    ·III. 21. Henry D. Smith died unmarried.

II. 10. Ann Loxley married Rev. Morgan John Rhees; had
    III. 24. Mary Rhees married Rev. Timothy Jackson.
    III. 25. Morgan J. Rhees married Grace Evans.
    III. 23. Benjamin Rush Rhees married Margaret G. Evans.
    III. 22. John Loxley Rhees married Rebecca McElwee.
    III. 26. Eliza Rhees married Rev. Nicholas Murray.

    III. 22. John Loxley Rhees married Rebecca McElwee.
          (See III. 1. Rhees family).
    III. 23 Dr. Benj. Rush Rhees married Margaret G. Evans.
          (See III. 2. Rhees family).
    III. 24. Mary Rhees married Rev. Timothy Jackson.
          (See III. 3. Rhees family.)
    III. 25. Rev. Morgan John Rhees married Grace Evans.
          (See III. 4. Rhees family.)
    III. 26. Eliza Rhees married Rev. Nicholas Murray.
          (See III. 5. Rhees family.)
II. 11. George Washington Loxley married Ann Taylor; had
III. 27. Rev. Benjamin Reed Loxley married J. Hopkins; had
    IV. 12. Ann Rhees Loxley married Rev. Robert Lowry.
    IV. 13. Elizabeth Jones Loxley married Henry B. Moore.
          (First husband).
    IV. 13. Elizabeth Jones Loxley married James M. Taylor.
          (Second husband).
    IV. 14. George Boardman Loxley, died unmarried.
    IV. 15. Benjamin Ogden Loxley married Tacie A. Evans.
          (First wife).
    IV. 15. Benjamin Ogden Loxley married Tacie Morgan.
          (Second wife).
III. 12. Eleanor Jones married Edward Duval; had
    IV. 1. William Jones Duval.
    IV. 2. Marcellus Duval.
    IV. 3. Gabriel B. Duval married Julia Nesbit.
    IV. 4. Octavia Duval married R. C. W. Radford.
III. 17. Charlotte Jones married Cyrus T. Smith; had
    IV. 5. William Jones Smith, died unmarried.
    IV. 6. Henry D. Smith, married.
    IV. 7. Lloyd Smith, died unmarried.
    IV. 8. Cyrus T. Smith, married.

IV. 9. Gertrude Smith, died unmarried.
IV. 10. Uselma C. Smith married,
IV. 11. Lloyda Smith died unmarried.
III. 19. Cyrus T. Smith, married Charlotte Jones.
        (See III. 17. Loxley family).
IV. 15. Benjamin Ogden Loxley, married Tacie A. Evans; had
    V. 1. Charles Evans Loxley, married.
    V. 2. Morris James Loxley, married.*

---

*The records of the Rhees and Loxley families were sent me by Mr. William J. Rhees, Smithsonian Institution, Washington, D. C. In his note to me, dated Washington, October 3d, 1898, he says: "I have at last completed a list of the descendants of Rev. Morgan John Rhees, and hope it will be of service to you * * * I have omitted dates of births, deaths and marriages to save space. Yours truly,
WM. J. RHEES.

Lowry Family.

Rev. Morgan John Rhees, Sr., married a daughter of Col. Benjamin Loxley (probably in Philadelphia), who was an officer in the Revolutionary War.

Some ot the children of Col. Benjamin Loxley were:

1. Geo. Washington Loxley, whose wife's name was Ann Taylor and who died in Philadelphia in 1865, at the age of 86.
2. Ann, who married a Rhees.
3. Jane, who married a Clark.
4. Betsey, who married a Jones.

From George Washington Loxley came the Rev. Benjamin Loxley, who married Mary Jackson Hopkins, and who died in Philadelphia, in 1865.

From the Rev. Benjamin Reed Loxley came:

1. Anna Rhees Loxley.
2. Elizabeth Jones Loxley.
3. George Boardman Loxley, died.
4. Benjamin Ogden Loxley.

Anna Rhees Loxley was married to the Rev. Robert Lowry, and died in 1890.

From the Rev. Robert Lowry and Anna Rhees Loxley came:

1. Rev. Harry Moore Lowry.
2. Wheaton Smith Lowry.
3. Robert Hanson Lowry, and two who died in infancy.

From the Rev. Harry Moore Lowry and Mary McAnale came:

1. May Lowry. who died.

From Robert Hanson Lowry and Lizzie Darling came:

1. Clarence Loxley Lowry, who died.
2. Edith Elizabeth Lowry.

Plainfield, New Jersey, September 19th, 1898. Rev. Robert Lowry, D. D.

Morgan John Rhees, Jr., D. D.

CHAPTER XI.

"Morgan John Rhees, Jr , D. D., was born at Somerset, Pa., Oct. 25, 1802. On reaching twenty-one he studied law under the celebrated David Paul Brown, of Philadelphia, and after being called to the bar he soon secured a respectable standing in his profession. In 1827 the Saviour found him, and 'chosen of him ere time began, he chose him in return,' and was baptized into the fellowship of the First Baptist Church of Philadelphia. He was ordained in September, 1829. His first fields of labor were Bordentown and Trenton, New Jersey. While in New Jersey he assisted in the formation of the State Convention for Missions, and was its Secretary from its organization until he left the state. In 1840 he accepted the invitation of its Board to become Corresponding Secretary of the Baptist Publication Society. In February, 1843, he took charge of the Second Baptist Church of Wilmington, Delaware; of this church he retained the oversight for seven years, during which he baptized nearly 300 persons. In 1850 he became pastor of the First Church of Williamsburg, N. Y., where he died January 15, 1853. He received the degree of Doctor of Divinity from the University of Rochester in 1852. Dr. Rhees was greatly blessed in every pastorate, and he rendered valuable services to the Publication Society. His calls to churches seek ing the best gifts were numerous. He had a fine intellect, the polish of a gentleman, the courage of a brave man, the piety of a saint, and the tenderness of a woman. He was loved by many hundreds while he lived, and his memory is still revered by the churches for which he labored, and by many admiring friends " (Rev. W. Cathcart, D. D., in "the Baptist Encyclopedia.")

Dr. R. B. Cook, in his history of the Delaware Baptists, in his reference to Dr. Rhees' pastorate of the Second Church, Wilmington, says:—"For seven years, Rev. Morgan J. Rhees, D. D., was their pastor, dur ing whose pastorate the church reached a membership of four hundred, and showed great liberality in their contributions to the various objects of benevolence. One year they report one thousand dollars contributed for benevolence abroad. Besides, they became self-sustaining, giving up voluntarily the aid extended them by the American Baptist Home Mission Society. In 1848, while pastor here, Dr. Rhees was made Moderator of the Philadelphia Association."

William Jones Rhees, a grandson of Morgan John Rhees.

CHAPTER XII.

WILLIAM JONES RHEES.

Smithsonian Institution. Born, Philadelphia, Pa., March 13, 1830.

Son of Benjamin Rush Rhees, M. D., and Margaret Grace (Evans) Rhees.
Grandson of Rev. Morgan John Rhees and Ann (Loxley) Rhees.
Great-grandson of BENJAMIN LOXLEY and Catharine (Cox) Loxley.
Grandson of Evan Rice Evans and Grace (Wallis) Evans.
Great-grandson of EVAN EVANS and Margaret (Nivin) Evans.
Great-grandson of Joseph Jacob Wallis and Elizabeth (Lukens) Wallis.
Great-great-grandson of JOHN LUKENS and Sarah (Lukens) Lukens.

Maj. Benjamin Loxley (1720-1801), of Philadelphia, Pennsylvania, Keeper of the King's stores in Philadelphia; resigned to assist the cause of Independence; a reward was offered for his head by the British Government; Delegate to Provincial Convention, Philadelphia, January 23-28, 1775; organized and was Captain of the 1st Artillery Company of Patriots in the American Army, Philadelphia, Colonel Samuel Mifflin, July, 1776; marched his company to Amboy, New Jersey, July 21, 1776; promoted to Mayor, August, 1776; at Germantown, Red Bank, Valley Forge, etc.; Member of Philadelphia Committee of Safety, 1774-1776; Delegate to Carpenter's Hall Conference, June 18th, 1776; made brass mortars, howitzers, traveling shops and fireworks for the Continental Army; gave instructions in the use of cannon and small arms to the Philadelphia Militia in the State House yard; much of his property was destroyed by the British Army when it occupied Philadelphia. It was in his house, known as the "Loxley House," that Lydia Darrach overheard the plans of the British officers and communicated them to Washington.

Col. Evan Evans (1732-1794), of Chester County, Pennsylvania, on Committee of Observation of Chester County Associators, December 20th, 1774; Member of Provincial Conference at Carpenter's Hall, Philadelphia, June 18th, 1776, which appointed and instructed the delegates in Congress from Pennsylvania to vote for independence;

Member of Convention, 1776, which framed the first constitution of the State; commanded 2d Battalion, Chester County Associators, 1776–1777; at battle of Trenton; Justice of Court of Common Pleas, Chester County, April 10th, 1777; organized 2d battalion of militia and made Colonel, May 7th, 1777; in battle of Brandywine, September 11th, 1777; Member of Pennsylvania Assembly, 1780–1783; Member of Council of Censors, 1783; Member of Supreme Executive Council of the State when Franklin was President, 1785.

John Lukens (1720–1789), of Philadelphia, Pennsylvania, appointed Surveyor-General for Pennsylvania by the Proprietary Government, December 8th, 1761, and by the State Council of Safety, 1776, continued until his death, 1789; one of the Commissioners to run the boundaries of New York, Pennsylvania, New Jersey; and for extending Mason and Dixon's Line, 1781.

William Jones Rhees was born in Philadelphia March 13th, 1830. He was a son of Benjamin Rush Rhees, M. D., and Margaret Grace (Evans) Rhees. His father was an eminent physician of Philadelphia, who was one of the founders of Jefferson Medical College, and a dean of the faculty. Mr. Rhees is a descendant of Revolutionary sires on both father and mother's side, and takes a great interest in the society of the "Sons of the American Revolution," being one of the charter members. Mr. Rhees is a graduate of the Philadelphia High School, from which he received the degree of A. M., in 1852. He was active in school societies and in amateur journalism. In 1847 he went to Meadville, Pennsylvania, and took a position as clerk and draughtsman in the Holland Land Company's office; was appointed a clerk in the census office in Washington in 1850, and, although, only twenty, had charge of the "Division of Social Statistics," or those relating to religion, schools, libraries, etc., with a large force of clerks under him.

While in the census office he acted as Secretary of the "Executive Committee" of the United States on the Industrial Exhibition in London in 1851, and had charge of business relative to exhibits made by Americans in this first great World's Fair. In 1853 Mr. Rhees was appointed Chief Clerk of the Smithsonian Institution and Private Secretary to Professor Joseph Henry, which positions he held until the latter's death. He continued as Chief Clerk under Professor Baird, and under a special Act of Congress, and appointed by Chief Justice Waite was acting Secretary of the Institution whenever Prof. Baird was absent. He has published a "Manual of Public Libraries" which is still the standard authority, a "Life of Smithson" and two large volumes of "Documents relative to the origin and history of the Smithsonian Institution," Guide-books to the Institution and Museum and other works. He was an active member of the Masonic Fraternity; Master of the Lebanon lodge; member of the Grand Lodge of the District, and Recorder of Washington Commandery Knights, a Templar for several years; he has always been a decided temperance man; one of the founders of "Metropolitan Division Sons of Temperance," composed wholly of government clerks: was Grand Worthy Patriarch of the order; established "Cadets of Temperance," "Bands of Hope," etc.

He was one of the three original founders of the "Young Men's Christian Association," and has held every office in it from Librarian to President; also as delegate to many national conventions. As teacher and superintendent of Sunday Schools, both church and Miss on, he is well known as an earnest worker, thorough organizer and liberal supporter. He had the management of many courses of popular lectures, and met and accompanied Professor John Tyndall on his visit to the United States. He has been a trustee of public schools, during the war and subsequently, for the old Second District, and also for the country, and had important chairmanships; prepared a history of the District relative to education manuals of the Board, and has taken active interest in the erection of new school houses, and the improvement of the system. For many years he was correspondent on special topics for various newspapers. He was a charter member of the Church of the Covenant (Presbyterian). Mr Rhees has for some years resided in the suburbs at his beautiful country seat, "Oakmont," and on account of delicate health, has not mingled lately in public affairs, nor active work outside of his official duties at the Smithsonian. Mr. Rhees has a large following of devoted friends and admirers, who are strongly attached to him by his high standard of honor, his gentle disposition and his inate gentility." (From "The Public Service," Washington, D. C., November 26, 1891).

Here is a worthy descendant of noble ancestors. In a private letter to the writer, dated Washington, D. C., Nov. 21, 1898, Mr. Rhees says:— "My proudest distinction is to have had such worthy Christian ancestors, and to have humbly, but faithfully, endeavored to follow their example."

An Appendix.

CHAPTER XIII.

After having arranged the materials of the preceding chapters, and given them to the printer, I received a large manuscript from Mr. Wm. J. Rhees (Washington), which had been written by Morgan J. Rhees after he had landed in America, in which, in the form of letters to a friend, he describes his remarkable tour on horseback through the South and the Northwestern Territory. The first letter is dated: "New York, October 21, 1794." It begins as follows:—

"DEAR FRIEND:—You expect a long letter ; I shall say as much as I can in a few words. Time flyeth—the tide of human affairs will not wait a moment; sufficient for my day are the occupation thereof. Having escaped the political tempest of my native country, I cheerfully submitted to the mercy of the waves, and with a fine breeze swelling the sails left Liverpool the 1st of August. In the greatest dangers I could sing:

> Let both the sea and tempest roar,
> And waves drive on from shore to shore;
> The whole Creation may be dark,
> The ocean swell like mountains high;
> And murm'ring billows kiss the sky—
> Hope is my anchor, God my ark.

The voyage turned out a long one (73 days), but I became so accustomed to my situation that I scarcely wished to see the shore. I was fully employed in reading and writing."

The most of this first letter is devoted to the giving of instructions to any who might have a desire to emigrate to America. Among the last words of this letter he says : "Next week I intend to commence my tour through the United States, South and Northwestern Territories. I shall endeavor to make such observations on the country, the laws, customs, manners and religion of the inhabitants as will give you some faint idea of the present state of America."

From this letter we see that he landed in New York about October 12, 1794. It also shows the substance and purpose of all the following letters, which we publish, word for word, as they were written by their illustrious author. Many things written in these letters may seem strange to the reader as he thinks of them in the light of present sentiments and customs, but they should be looked at in the light of the times in which they were written, and lead us to think of the marvelous changes and progress made within only a century.   THE AUTHOR.

(Letter 2d.)

NEW YORK, October 29th, 1794.

DEAR SIR:—I forgot to mention in my last, the pleasing sensations which I felt whilst sailing from Sandy Hook between Long and Staten Islands up to New York—the buildings on both sides the bay, modest and neat—Governor's Island and York City in front, formed a most beautiful landscape. The North and East Rivers, opening their arms as it were to embrace York Island, as the beloved spot where they intend to deposit their stores, even the treasures of the East and the West, the North and the South. The whole island, which is about 15 miles in length, and on the average about 2½ in breadth, will, it is probable, in the course of time, be covered with houses and stores; upwards of eleven hundred houses have been erected this year, some of them very elegant and commodious. The city is between four and five miles in circumference, and contains about 40,000 inhabitants. The increase of population is almost incredible—emigrants from all parts are flocking in, consisting principally of Germans, Irish, French, Scotch and English. The last, by what I can learn from them, are very much attached to this city; it is certainly an excellent situation for commerce, but the land in general throughout the state is not easy of cultivation, being hilly, stony and heavily timbered. The Chenessee country and some other parts are an exception. The soil there is deemed very rich, but the inhabitants are subject to agues and lake fevers.

New York being the Capital of and the only port in the State will, of course, be the emporium of a great extent of country. When the Western Posts shall be delivered up by the British, this place in a great measure will command the commerce of the lakes. It is expected that a conveyance by water will soon be obtained to the Ohio and Mississippi; the land carriage at present is but short, tide water runs up above Albany, which is 160 miles from hence. Thence the navigation proceeds up the Mohawk River to Lake Ontario, without any other interruption than two short portages, one at the little falls of half a mile, round which they are now cutting a canal, the other of one mile at Fort Stanwix, about one hundred miles west of Shenectady, which is a little town on the banks of the Mohawk, inhabited chiefly by low Dutch. The land on this river is generally esteemed good. From Fort Stanwix they descend with the current to Oswego, one hundred miles more to the west, where the British hold a post at the entrance of Lake Ontario. From Oswego, vessels sail to Niagara, Kingston and any other port on the lake. Kingston is a new town on the northeast corner of Lake Ontario, where the lake empties itself and forms the River St. Lawrence, the banks of which are thick-settled down to Lake St. Francois, where the Provinces of Upper and Lower Canada are divided. This river is navigable for vessels of one hundred tons and upwards to Oswegatche, 70 miles from Kingston, but vessels seldom go down the river, as the fort at Kingston serves as a deposit for all the public stores, provision and merchandise for the upper ports; from Kingston they sail to Niagara across the lake, which may be called a little sea. The mouth of the Niagara River (between the fort and the town called Newark) is said to afford a safe and commodious harbor, large enough for half the British Navy.

Besides Newark, there are several important situations in this part of the country. The landing places at each end of the portage—Fort Erie, the Head of Lake Ontario, and York, called by the natives, Torrento. The lower landing or

Queenston is about seven miles up the river from Newark, where the vessels discharge their cargoes and take in furs, collected from one to three thousand miles back. Vessels of sixty and hundred tons unload here, and the goods are carried in wagons to the upper landing place or Chippawa Creek, three miles past the great falls. From Chippawn, the merchandise is transported in Batteaux to Fort Erie, and shipped there on board of vessels for Detroit and Michilimakinac. You have no doubt read of the Falls of Niagara, that famous Cataract whose grandeur and sublimity baffles every description. Above these Falls is likewise a spring emitting a gas of inflammable air, which, confined in a pipe, and a flame applied to it, will boil the water of a tea kettle in fifteen minutes.

In these settlements the Parliament of Great Britain has renounced forever the power of taxation. Had they done this twenty-five years ago to the United States they would have spared much blood and treasure. But consistency is not to be expected in your Cabinet. I am afraid they never think of doing a virtuous act 'till they are obliged to do it.

Excuse me for this long digression; the situation of New York led me to do it. You will be able from what I have said to form an idea of the inland navigation of this country. The river St. Lawrence is navigable 500 miles from the sea for vessels of 600 tons burthen, and all the Western rivers head near the lakes, so that in a short time the merchandise of Europe will be conveyed to every port of the Western water cheaper than it can be carried from here to Pittsburg.

In forming our settlement I have three or four things particularly in view—a healthy situation, an advantageous location for commerce, a rich soil and a good neighborhood. The internal government likewise is better in some States than others. In this State, Negro slavery is tolerated that I do not approve of. A citizen preacher has not the same privilege with a citizen cobler, that I don't like. By a strange infatuation several of the States to the southward, and New York to the northward have enacted that a preacher shall not be elected to any civil office, legislative or judicial. This would be very right if the States paid them, but the laws in America know no such men as the clergy, and of course should make no distinction between them and other citizens. It will not be so long; it was a stretch of zeal to banish the power of priests from Legislative Assemblies, and as the toleration of slavery, it cannot last long in any country. The Day Star from on high has risen—the morning dawns—the sun appears—the remains of slavery shall be soon swept from the new world with the bosom of pure democracy.

I have been on Long Island, which is 140 miles in length, and on a medium, about ten in breadth—some of the land is level and fertile, but a great deal stony and broken.

I took an excursion of three or four days on the continent; the country was in many places picturesque and capable of great improvements. Mount Pleasant, 36 miles from York, is likely to become a place of some importance.* I was very much

*A town called Sparta has been laid out adjoining this place, by some British Republicans. It has a capital landing place—a natural rock forms a pier in the river where sloops and even ships may load and unload. It is to be wished these Sons of Freedom may be successful in their attempt to form a settlement, but from its proximity to New York, I am fearful they will find it difficult to establish any considerable trade at their American Sparta.

pleased with the hospitality of the inhabitants, but upon the whole I think the yeomanry too buckish; it is no harm, they should know and feel their consequence, but affectation and pride is despicable in every character; even domestics will not be called servants. You cannot offend them more than by asking them "Is your Master at home?" Do not these adhere strictly to the command of Christ, "Call no man Master?"

New York is deemed the gayest place in America. It is said the ladies in the richness and brilliancy of their dress are not equalled in any city in the United States. But plumes and feathers, in my opinion, are no ornament to Republican women. However, they are not solely employed in attentions to dress, but are studious to add the more brilliant and lasting accomplishments of the mind." In company the other day, when observing what madness it would be for England to run the risk of a war with the United States, a lady exclaimed: "What! Great Britain conquer America! No; we might take up that Little Island and plunge her into one of our lakes!"

If the American women have imbibed such a noble spirit, what are you to expect from the men? There are complaints, however, that New York abounds with English Aristocrats and American Tories; but before the great mass of Republicans they dwindle to nothing. Should they, according to their never-ceasing custom, endeavor to infringe on the rights of the people, the Americans have only to place them in such a situation, as not to be able to tyrannize over their fellow-men.

Since the Revolution, the literature of the State has engaged the attention of the Legislature, and some excellent regulations have been made, so that it is expected in a short time, that every child, poor as well as rich, will be instructed to read, write and keep accounts in the English tongue.

Columbia College, in this city, is established on a very liberal plan, and likely to be the seat of scientific knowledge. There are likewise in the State many Academies, which will no doubt be the nurseries of great and virtuous characters. In a free country, the mind, if not early corrupted, rises to refined elegance; unshackled by superstition, it soars through universal space, collects the aetherial blossoms of Paradise, and forms a treasure of knowledge superior to the rubies of the East, or the topaz of Ethiopia.

As to religion in this city and State, I cannot say much of it at present. No sect has an incentive to envy the other for superior privileges. Yet there is not that cordiality I would wish to see among men professing to be the disciples of the meek and humble Jesus. Alas! human nature is the same in every part of the world, and prejudice of education is not removed in a day or a twelve month, particularly where men find it their interest to keep it up. However, the time is fast approaching when prejudice must yield to truth; dispassionate enquiry supersede intemperate declamation, and private interest give way to the public weal.

The different denominations are classed under the names of English Presbyterians, Dutch Reformed, Baptist, German Lutheran, Episcopalians, Friends or Quakers, Moravians, Methodists, Roman Catholics and Jews. When Oh! my friend shall those names be ground to powder by the little stone cut out of the Mountain without hands, and the names of Christ alone be mentioned as our leader to everlasting glory?　　　　　　　　　　　　　　Adieu: I remain ever yours,

　　　　　　　　　　　　　　　　　　　　　　　　　　　　M. J. R.

(Letter 3d.)

DEAR FRIEND:—A farther description of the republic of New York must be omitted 'till my return. I shall just inform you of an useful institution lately established there for the information and assistance of persons emigrating from foreign countries—a similar society is formed at Philadelphia. Emigrants on their first arrival would do well to apply to the officers of these humane and truly philanthropic societies for such information as they may stand in need of. The industrious laborer and useful mechanic will immediately be directed where to find employment, such as may be in distress will recognize in every member of this fraternity a friend and a brother—happy asylum for the distressed of all nations! Here the wolf and the lamb, the leopard and the kid, the calf and the young lion and the fatling live together, and a child at the head of a free government may lead them to liberty and peace.

Oh! that I could stretch forth a brother's hand and draw my oppresed countrymen from their ecclesiastical and royal prisons to this hospitable shore that they might sacrifice a free-will offering in the temple of freedom which rises in the new world magnificently fair; that they may behold its collossal pillars, and with transports of joy, adore the universal parent within its dome. Under the shade of the tree of Liberty, we may traverse this continent, and notwithstanding the blast of tyrants its branches will soon cover the globe.

I march on and across the North river, at Powel's Hook, from thence through the mosquito marshes, a salt meadow about thirty miles in length and three and one-half in breadth, which when properly drained and improved will be a great acquisition to York. At present the hay is very course and cannot be conveyed from the ground where it remains in stacks 'till the frozen hand of winter binds the swampy soil. We crossed over the ferries of Hakensak and Posaik,* two rivers which run in a serpentine form through this meadow. Here you may see sloops sailing in different directions without seeing their hulks. You might suppose they were driven by the wind on dry land, for owing to the eveness of the earth, the rivers are kept out of sight 'till you ascend the hill near Newark, a neat little town which in miniature is emblematic of every thing modest and sublime in this rising republic. From Newark I proceeded to Elizabeth town where I rested a night at a friend's house which was filled with freedom and hospitality. This is a scattered little town containing about 150 houses and some public buildings. The situation is agreeable, and the soil in the neighborhood fertile.

From thence to Scot's Plain, where I observed a singular instance of American liberality. Whilst at a place of worship on Sunday, a company of Friends (which in Britian are more commonly called Quakers) entered the house and took their seats. I thought this rather strange, for in your country that sect seldom associate with other denominations. I was still more surprised when I heard the minister of the place address them thus at the close of the service : "Friends, I am glad to see you here. I give you the same liberty as the Disciples had in ancient time; wherefore,

---

*Since writing the above, elegant bridges have been erected over them. The cataract in the Posaik merits notice. The descent is upwards of seventy feet perpendicular which occasions a cloud of vapour to arise that adds beauty to the scene, and elevates the mind of the admiring traveller.

men and brethren, if you have a word of exhortation to the people, say on. A public Friend among them immediately arose and addressed the congregation very affectionately for fifteen or twenty minutes. Even Episcopalians in this country will invite what are called dissenters to preach for them; but in America there are no dissenters; the curse of religious establishments has been banished from the land; the inhabitants have made a noble barter; they enjoy in its stead all the blessings which are forever flowing from the Fountain of Freedom. Free enquiry after truth and a candid investigation of every subject, is a natural consequence in the system of equality, here a man may do both without suffering in his person or property.

Wherever I meet with a pulpit which is not open to all men of moral conduct and abilities, I conclude that Mrs. Superstition is housekeeper and Messrs. Prejudice and Bigotry the doorkeepers. What then! shall naked Truth dread the Drapery of Error? No; although "her head is filled with dew and her locks with the drops of the night," divine lustre shines around her temple—she moves on in the majesty of her mind towards the meridian day of her glory.

The verdure and prospect as I approached the banks of the Raritan about two miles above N. Brunswick is not to be exceeded by many parts in Britain. This city is situated on the south side of the Raritan, over which a capital bridge is now building. It contains near three hundred houses, a college and two places for public worship; were it built on the hill instead of the low bottom where it now stands, it would be more likely to rise to importance. Every attempt to make Amboy a place of note has proved abortive, although it has one of the finest harbors on the continent and is agreeably situated on a pleasant neck of land at the mouth of Raritan.

At N. Brunswick I left the Philadelphia road to the right, of course, could not see Princeton and Trenton—the latter is at present the Capital of the State. I tarried one night at Hight's Town (a little village) and proceeded to Bordentown, pleasantly situated on the banks of the Delaware. Here Paine wrote his famous pamphlet called "Common Sense." After viewing Allison's Academy, where a great number of young men are educated in all the useful and ornamental branches of literature, I pursued my route to Burlington, lying partly on an island, and partly on the Delaware. Some of the streets are spacious and ornamented with trees regularly arranged.

Before I quit New Jersey I must give you a summary view of it. The lands are good, bad and indifferent, but the worst is calculated for good orchards. It is reported that this State produces some of the best cider in the world. I have drank some very good, but I believe sufficient care is not taken to preserve the apple district according to their kind and separate the sound from the rotten. Notwithstanding this is a cider country—there are many of the first taverns where you can procure any either in bottles or out of the cask. It is rather a disgrace to the publicans not to encourage the sale of their own produce.

Manufacturers in general in this Commonwealth are at a low ebb; however, the iron works are a source of great wealth to it. The cotton manufactory at Patterson is expected in time to produce something considerable, but unless the State Legislatures and the Federal Government will combine their influence and support, the British merchant, notwithstanding the present duties on imports, will undersell the American Manufacturer. The difference between the price of labor in the two countries, is more than the freight and duty put together.

It is not British articles that the Americans have to dread, but British influence, which will naturally be imported with them. It will creep in imperceptibly with those English agents who have nothing to lose, but everything to get from their connection with the old country.

The inhabitants of the United States should, therefore, if they are determined to establish their independence, strain every nerve to patronize their manufactural as well as agricultural interest. It is truly surprising that Congress should be so blind to the welfare of their country as to levy an excise upon any of their home productions. This bad law has already produced a kind of insurrection among the whiskey boys in the four western counties of Pennsylvania. Some argue if the citizens on the sea coast have to pay duty on foreign spirits, that their brethren in the remote parts of the Union should likewise support government by paying excise on their own manufactures. This species of reasoning may do very well as it regards the interest of a few individuals, but as it respects the well-being of the nation it can have no weight. It is true the aggregate sum of the taxes of this country will not amount to half the money spent upon W——s by the king's household in England. It was therefore a piece of mischievous madness to rebel against laws made by the representatives of a free people. Should they err through ignorance or be misguided by undue influence, their constituents have it in their power to change them at pleasure. However, when the whole truth of this affair is known I expect it will appear none other than an aristocratical bubble, bursting its vengence on the heads of a few peaceable remonstrants. The intriguers of the plot, if not found in the act of accusing the innocent, will probably make their escape, whilst the pure patriots who fought and bled in the cause of freedom, may be insulted by a few beardless boys wantonly exercising their authority under the influence of a monarchical minister. The seed of aristocracy always produces the weeds of anarchy. How far taxes—even upon luxuries may counteract vice or whether they retard its progress at all, are questions which I am not at present prepared to answer. This I know that justice and liberty will forever proclaim "Let property be taxed[3] and all persons of good morals be represented." The moment we deviate from this principle, we verge towards despotism; corruption creeps in like a snail before it flows like a flood; a nation like Britain may flourish perhaps for a century or more, whilst it continues gradually to enact laws which in the end will inevitably annihilate its government. We cannot therefore be too watchful in guarding our rights, for righteousness alone continues to exalt a nation. Righteousness is the basis of Peace, the protector of commerce, the Alpha and Omega of liberty, wherefore I shall remain its advocate.

Burlington, November, 1794.   M. J. R.

---

*Shipley saith "In whatever hands the power of taxation is lodged, it implies all other powers. Arbitrary taxation is plunder authorized by law. It is the support and essence of tyranny and has done more mischief to mankind than those other three scourges from Heaven—famine, pestilence and the sword.

92

(Letter 4th.)

DEAR SIR:—My last letter left you abruptly at Burlington. I am sorry I could not lead you to Nassau Hall at Princeton to view the college, where the philosophic Smith presides. I crossed the Delaware at Dunk's Ferry. On entering Pennsylvania the face of the country, I think, changed for the better. The Pennsylvanians, it is said, excel all their brethren in the Union in agricultural improvement, mechanical inventions and manufactural applications.

The citizens of the United States cannot in all things imitate the Europeans. In farming the difference of soil and expense of manuring must be consulted. The same principles in the two countries may produce different effects; new experiments must be made, and the most successful attempts followed. The plaister of Paris has been introduced with some success so as to obtain immediate crops, but li..e other incentives without proper care in the management of the ground, it will leave the soil weaker. The mixture of clay with sand, the more common introduction of seed, watering the meadows, &c, will give a different aspect to the country. A register of American improvements, with the observations of travelers, would perhaps be of greater utility to the farmer than cart-loads of European books on husbandry. Such books are doubtless useful and our countrymen, provided they can bring laborers with them, will not fail to make a good fortune by farming in America. The high price of labor, and the difficulty of procuring workmen at any rate, are the greatest obstacles to be surmounted. The poor and many of the rich are continually migrating to the westward, where they can procure lands cheap and in a short time become independent. Wages cannot be expected to reduce much in the Atlantic States 'till the tide of population cease to flow over the Appalachian Mountains.

I believe it is a general error among American farmers to grasp at too much land ; purchasers lay out their money in procuring a greater tract than they can conveniently cultivate. The expectations of getting rich by the advance in the price of lands will be a strong barrier against reformation. There are some, however, who pay particular attention to manuring and arranging their farms into useful and elegant order. In a country which offers so many temptations to the speculating tribe, it is not to be wondered at that many should be led by the cupidity of their hearts to make such essays towards corruption as will involve themselves and the country in some difficulties ; like the miser who vociferates "More money, more money still," these terrestrial monsters are continually seeking after more lands. High mountains and extensive plains they hug in their arms, and anxiously look forward for some new spot, that they may pay additional homage to their dusty God.

After spending a few days in the township of Lower Dublin, I passed through Frankfort to the City of Brotherly Love. The country in its vicinity is nearly level, and such an extent of it in a state of cultivation that the superior advantages this place possesses over New York are readily perceived in regard to a fine back country—vast tracts of unlocated lands, numerous beds of coal, mines and mill-seats open a fine field for the industrious and enterprising spirit. The exports from this city are greater by far than any port in the Union, notwithstanding the malignant scourge (yellow fever) which visited the inhabitants in 1793, the place is fast rising to eminence ; its market, not without reason, has been numbered by travellers among the first in the world ; the streets are both elegant and eligible for dispatch of business; some of the buildings vie in neatness with the first in Europe; its charitable and public institutions do honor to the American character; the penal laws are an example of philanthropy to all mankind; its prisons may justly be called a House of Reformation and all the prisoners, manufacturers—in it none can be idle; such as have no trade are instructed in some useful art, whereby they are enabled to support themselves and even save money; the sexes are kept separate; the time of imprisonment is apportioned to the crime; none suffer death but for wilful murder; all are supplied with plenty of good provisions and healthy apartments, but no strong liquors will be admitted within the walls of this bettering mansion. Time would fail to enumerate the excellency of its hospitals, libraries and museum, which although in an infant state, represent the country under the simile of a well-constructed garden, where all the seeds of virtue have been sown. They grow and flourish in their native soil—the soil of liberty.

When I have a leisure hour I attend the House of Representatives—the building is modest and neat. On the 19th the venerable President delivered his address to Congress on the state of the Union, etc. It contained an unhappy expression which will cause a comment not pleasing to the feelings of the first magistrate and his friends "Self created societies," these were the objectionable words, and applied no doubt to the Democratic societies in this country, who are violent against the excise laws—steady in their remonstrances against Britain, and enthusiastic in their attachment to France. The President, although brave as Caesar in battle, yet is not a sanguinary man. The enormous excesses of French massacres might have damped for the moment his accustomed ardor for liberty. It is sometimes difficult to trace disagreeable effects to their source. The human mind generally yields to the first impressions, and sometimes, though not often, errs through excess of Philanthropy. If we err at all it is the safest side, but in a war of elements like that of France, where a long arrear of Protestant blood was to be avenged—so many ignoble despots and vagabond priests, to be reduced to men, else banished or destroyed. The divine thunder, which had long been reserved must be tremendous, and the electrical shocks which purified the air of such vermin, rapid and severe. What we lament most is, that in pulling down the strong-holds of tyranny, so many of the first-born sons of freedom should be destroyed in the ruins!

But you'll ask me "What has all this to do with your account of Philadelphia?" Much, my brother—in every respect. What are improperly called "French Principles," pervade the universe and universal emancipation must be the result. Notwithstanding the Americans did much in the cause of freedom, they stumbled as it regards the poor Africans at the threshold of equal rights. Although there are but few temporary slaves in this State, whilst one remains it will be a disgrace to the country. The abolition societies are zealous, and its members numerous. They intend bringing the important question to an issue before the supreme court "whether it be consonant with the Constitution to hold any human being in bondage." The Heavens above and the earth beneath say no. If the jury should say, yes, I wish they might have their residence for a few months with the Dey of Algiers in order to taste the sweets of slavery. It would do your heart good to behold the African school with their place of worship in this city; the children, considering their circumstances, make great proficiencies; they have certainly equal abilities with the whites, but whilst the prejudice of the age is so much in favor of the latter, it will militate very much against mental improvement of the former.

Literature advances in this Republic with its increasing population and the flood of wealth which continually flows into the coffers of the State. It is expected that in addition to the present university and seminaries, schools will be established and supported at the expense of the public throughout the Commonwealth.

The Pennsylvanians are convinced that a republican government cannot be supported without virtue and knowledge ; ignorance and vice are always the forerunners of royalty and the only pillars which uphold earthly monarchy—wherever the true light shines, king and priestcraft will flee from thence, to the dark corners of the earth.

Paul exhorted the primitive Christians to pray for kings—certainly that their eyes might be opened to see the evil of absolute power ; this is implied in the annexed argument "that we may lead quiet and peaceable lives," a thing which despots will never grant if they can help it. Peter advised the disciples to "fear God," before they honored "the king." The best way to honor kings is by telling them their faults, and reprove them for their folly, as John the Baptist did Herod. Such conduct may be deemed high treason in some countries, but we have the command of Christ "When persecuted in one city, flee to the other."

I endeavored to prove, before I left Britain, that all who dissented from the established religion in that country, were persecuted by the Higher Powers, and that it was their duty, unless they could obtain equal liberty with the rest of their fellow citizens at home, to migrate to that country where they might enjoy their natural birth-right without fear or molestation ; I am still of the same opinion ; notwithstanding the difficulties you have to encounter in the way for the sake of liberty you should surmount them all ; and embark for America, where the persecuted Penn founded a city of refuge for the oppressed of all nations ; here religion has to demonstrate it's efficacy by the "force of argument instead of the argument of force."

If Christianity cannot be promulgated by voluntary supplies, it should not be supported at all. The general custom in this country is to collect after every sermon. The Deacons have each a pole about 6 feet long, at one end of which a velvet bag is fixed (not dissimilar to a well known emblem of liberty); in this they receive the free-will offerings of the congregation. It is usual, beside, in some churches, to let their pews ; others have subscriptions for the support of their ministers ; some don't pay their preachers at all—they think as the Gospel is free its ministration should be free also. Nothingarians can have no occasion to bark or complain, for the law extorts nothing from their pockets. A noble country for misers ! they may worship their mammon without any priest to consecrate their altars !

I must soon leave this flourishing city, which some suppose will be the largest in the world. Its inhabitants at present amount to about 60,000 ; formerly they had the character of being unsociable and less hospitable than their American brethren. I hope they have felt the reproof of traveling authors and are determined in future to excel, if possible, all others in acts of charity and deeds of mercy.

Much has been said in praise of the New York fair, but very little notice has been taken by writers on this subject of the Pennsylvania ladies. I suppose this must be owing to the latter's paying more attention to cultivate the mind, than adorn their persons, because they prefer family economy to female extravagance. Here they do not choose the foppery of fashion, and the butterfly frippery of courts—painting, plumes and feathers they leave to Indians and barbarians. "The mind, the mind is the standard of the man;" and why not of the woman?

The manners of the Friends, or Quakers, may appear stiff to strangers, but, in my opinion, honest simplicity is far preferable to polite hypocrisy. I must bid you adieu ; be assured I remain   Ever Yours,   M. J. R.

(Letter 5th.)

BALTIMORE, December, 1794.

DEAR SIR:—From Philadelphia I proceeded principally along the post road to this place. Here and there I wandered about to see the country and collect useful information. I rested the first night at Chichester or Marquis Hook, a little village on the banks of the Delaware. It is twenty miles from Philadelphia and five from Chester, the capitol of a county of that name in Pennsylvania, remarkable for being the place where the First Colonial Assembly met in 1682. It is a delightful morning's ride from the metropolis, and the road is much frequented by the Beau Mondi in the Spring and Summer seasons.

I enter the State of Delaware, one of the smallest in the Union, without having the most healthy clime or fertile soil—it has however local advantages. Its borders being washed by the delectable Delaware and the Atlantic ocean—the produce of some counties in Pennsylvania likewise pass through it to market.

The town of Wilmington is admirably situated on an eminence between Christiana and Brandywine Creeks from whence you have a magnificient view of the merchantmen and other vessels traversing the Delaware to and from the ocean. The town abounds with French emigrants from the West Indies. etc. Most articles are as dear as at Philadelphia. The mills on Brandywine (thirteen in number) justly merit the notice of travellers, as they are ranked with the first in the world. The mechanical O. Evans, has exceeded all the millwrights in his inventions to spare manual labor. From the sloop's deck to the upper loft—the screen and the binn, his machinery will convey the wheat with the touch of a finger. It progresses through the whole process of millery as it were by a perpetual motion; then descends in fine flour to the hold of the vessels, which conveys it to different parts of the world to support some virtuous republicans and many ungrateful aristocrats. Here are about 300,000 bushels of wheat and corn ground annually, but if constantly supplied with grain they are supposed capable of grinding 400,000. I passed through Christiana, another little town which stands on the ascent of a hill commanding a fine prospect, to Pencader, so called after a place of the same name in Carmarthenshire, South Wales. This is part of the Welsh tract formerly inhabited by some of our countrymen. There are but few even of their descendants there at present. The soil was perhaps too poor for them to procure a comfortable subsistence; they have removed to the South and West, and scattered over the continent. An old Welsh gentleman who resides here, and has travelled over all the Atlantic States has given me a particular account of their perigrinations from their first period of settlement to the present time.

Small and unimportant as this Commonwealth may appear, it sends two Senators to Congress as well as the largest and most populous States in the Union. This appears strange in the scale of equal representation, but they say it is to support the independence of each State this plan was adopted.

Of late the farmers have suffered considerably from the Hessian fly; it is astonishing what depredations this little insect has committed on the American grain; several attempts have been made to destroy it; the best remedy, according to some, is to sow late, for early in the Fall the flies come in such a body that you may as well endeavor to resist an army of Sans Culottes as to impede their progress. This scourge to the farmers does not visit all parts of the continent, nor the same neighborhood for many years together—they travel on from place to place like locusts without a king.

The staple commodity of this State is wheat. It is said that Philadelphia alone receives annually from its creeks about 270,000 barrels of flour; 300,000 bushels of wheat; 170,000 bushels of Indian corn, besides barley, oats, &c. but a great part of these articles are the produce of Pennsylvania. Its manufactures consist of paper, iron, snuff, glauber salts and magnesia. Apples, pears, peaches, plums, quinces and other small fruit grow in abundance.

I must quit the State of Delaware. The first town I came to on entering Maryland is Elkton, on the head of a navigable river called Elk. It is forty-nine miles south-west of Philadelphia from whence the roads are tolerable, with some good spots of land, but a great deal of pauvre soil.

From Elkton to Baltimore is sixty-nine miles; the greatest part of this country is barren, hilly and broken; there are a few exceptions and some eligible situations for towns, among the number is a little place called Charleston which commands a delightful prospect, from its elevated situation over Chesapeak Bay.

I crossed the serpentine Susquehanna at Havre, where it is about one mile broad. The town lies on a fine level bottom and contains forty houses. The country is picturesque about Bush Town and Abingdon, containing a few scattered houses and a Methodist College* at present unoccupied. The hills in many parts of this country are full of iron ore, but it requires to be ten times thicker settled before the hundredth part can be manufactured.

Travelling, in regard to expenses at Inns, is much the same here as in England; in some of them you are as well entertained; coach fare is much cheaper; beer and porter dearer. The Americans as yet have not paid that attention which they ought to the brewing of malt liquor. An exception may be made in favor of Philadelphia where there are already thirteen breweries which are said to consume upwards of 50,000 bushels of barley annually. The retailers of liquors likewise get an enormous profit. The publicans in most countries are fond of making rapid fortunes.

You may perceive by the map that Maryland possesses advantages in navigation equal to any of the United States. The Chesapeak, which is one of the largest bays in the world, runs through the heart of the Commonwealth. The Potomac also as it divides the State from Virginia, is navigable to George-Town and the Federal city.

---

*It has since been burnt.

Literature is encouraged and the different sects of Christians are zealous. Some among each to convert men to righteousness, others to proselyte to their different opinions. Annapolis, the seat of government, is a neat little city; the inhabitants hospitable and polite; the State House is the largest and most superb building in the United States; and the College daily increases in reputation. The following extract from an oration on the liberty of the press delivered last week by one of its students will give you an idea of the prevailing spirit among the American youth, and with what jealousy they watch the conduct of their magistrates.

After defining his subject and applying its possession to the State and Federal government, he pays a tribute of praise to the President and proceeds. "However estimable　＊　＊　＊

I hasten to give you a short account of Baltimore. There is an old man in the neighborhood who says "that within his memory all the inhabitants of the town consisted of an Irishman and his hut." According to the census taken in 1790 they consisted of 13,758 souls ; at present, it is supposed, they amount to 18,000. It is the largest and most flourishing port in the State, and ranks as the third in the Union. It is truly astonishing with what rapidity towns and cities rise in this country, thus whilst

> "The Eastern World enslaved its glory ends
> An Empire rises where the sun descends."

Here are ten places of worship, and as many different sects of religion living in peace and harmony ; nothing can be more demonstrative that full liberty of conscience is not inimical to the well-being of society and civil government.

Some parts of Baltimore are deemed unhealthy, but upon the whole it presents a beautiful prospect where health and hilarity may forever reign. Like most infantile places, some of the streets are as yet dirty, but others are well paved and fit for the feet of the ladies.

At Fell Point, below the town, the yellow fever raged this Fall. Its spread was attributed to a want of care and cleanliness among the poor Irish emigrants who resided principally in that quarter. Dr. Ramsey advises the Americans to banish from their shores the liquid fire of the West Indies. I would add, banish from your streets all the dirt and filth, from your pools all the stagnant waters ; let your rooms be whitewashed as often as possible during the summer heat, and adopt the French mode of living upon weak soups, which is perhaps as good an anti-epidemic as any yet prescribed.

It is evident from their conduct that many of the Baltimoreans are men of an enterprising spirit, but too many of the country people, I am afraid, are indolent in the extreme. The Marylanders in general have a sickly complexion—they may appear more so to me after being accustomed to the rosy cheeks in Cambria. 'If we form a righteous judgment we must not judge by outward appearance even of health.

I am happy to inform you that the culture of tobacco is on the decline ; it spunges the spirit and strength of the land, as well as the health of the planters. Wheat is become a substitue. This, instead of fumigating the brain, envigorates the body and enriches the possessor without impoverishing the soil.

The Kite-Foot Tobacco is said to be peculiar to this State; it is only the second and third leaves from the ground which soon grow to maturity and of course have less strength. The most common growth of trees are pine, sassafras, magnolia and various kinds of oak. Their orchards are inferior to none in the Union. Rye, whiskey and peach brandy are manufactured in large quantities, but wheat, Indian corn and tobacco are the staple commodities.

Although this State was originally settled by Roman Catholics, they had the good policy to grant universal freedom to all sects;* would to God its present inhabitants granted the same civil Liberty to all the human species. The existence of slavery in the United States is a degrading badge of their once having been British Colonies. England, although she boasts of having no slaves at home, permitted her Machiavilian merchants to ravage the deserts of Africa in order to cultivate the wilds of Columbia. The spirit of manumission, however, prevails—many have liberated their slaves, and more are likely to follow. That the words tolerance, intolerance and slavery may become obsolete in all the dictionaries of the world is the common prayer of   Yours, &c,   M. J. R.

(Letter 6th.)

RESPECTED FRIEND:—Just as I left Baltimore I met a Regiment of the Militia returning from their bloodless campaign in the western counties of Pennsylvania. They were received and saluted by their fellow citizens with every mark of esteem due to Volunteers who had sacrificed their time and ease to defend the sovereignty of the law; a law which the greatest part of them most probably were disgusted with, but in a country where any law may be repealed as soon as the public will is known. The love of order forbids the appearance of resistance to the civil magistrate.

How widely dissimilar the sensations in beholding this little army starting from their homes at the exigency of the moment to those I had been used to feel in viewing an host of slaves, commanded by despots to impede the progress of Liberty, and wreck their vengeance on their brethren of mankind. But "Hear Oh! ye Kings, give ear Oh! ye Princes" the artillery of Republicans shall batter down your towering castles. Open your eyes Oh! Tyrants and behold the irresistible energy of freemen. The stars in their courses shall fight for them, and the elements conspire to confound their adversaries. Be dispersed then ye standing armies; ye sinks of immortality be drained; ye dogs of war be scattered; ye heralds of slavery be gone. Behold the American eagle spreading her wings towards the rising sun, and bearing on her pinions the sons of freedom to the zenith of glory!

Oh! my friend I would wish to soar still higher but the roughness of the road and approach of night interrupted my meditation. I am come however to a friendly inn, the landlord of which freely entertains every description of the oratorial tribe.

Next morning I breakfasted at Brandenburg and immediately entered the Territory of Columbia, a tract of ten miles square ceded by the States of Maryland and Virginia for the seat of the Federal Government after the year 1800. The design of the city was drawn by the celebrated Major L. Enfant, which you have no doubt seen; the Junction of the Potomac and the eastern branch; spacious streets; numerous springs; variety of ascents, affording beautiful prospects are the prominent features which characterise the advantages of this place. There are as yet but few houses built; the walls of the Capitol are a few feet above ground; the President's

---

*This is a mistake, it was not even universal toleration.—John T. Griffith.

house is 280 feet in front by 275; and the grand hotel will soon be finished; George-Town which adjoins, stands on a number of little hills intersected by dingles running in every direction, forms an agreeable shade in the picture of the city; it contains about 240 houses besides public buildings; the inhabitants appear healthy and cheerful; the Union of the Roman Catholics and Protestants who have instituted an academy for the promotion of literature, is another instance proving that equal laws are the best means to remove prejudice and purge the augean stable of its rubbish; the Potomac is navigable thus far for ships; canals are cutting to avoid the different falls in the river. When those are completed this will probably be the cheapest route from the Atlantic to the Ohio. The soil in the adjacent country is indifferent.

Here I crossed the Potomac in my way to Alexandria a post of entry and post town of Virginia only eight miles from the Federal city. It contains about 500 house chiefly of brick and carries on a considerable trade to the West Indies and Europe. Here are a greater number of wagons bringing wheat and flour to market from the Shenandoah Valley and other places, than I have seen anywhere on the continent. I tarried in this town a few days and made some excursions into the neighboring country. The land has been everywhere reduced by tobacco. The people are friendly and hospitable, but do not appear to be the best farmers. This they acknowledge, and are willing to receive instructions. Emigrants from different parts have it in their power by example and enterprising spirit to give new life to the country.

On my road to Mount Vernon, some of the huts by the side of it appeared miserable, and still more distressed inhabitants. Oh! slavery it is thy complexion! Had the President of the United States been at home, I did not mean to address him as Dederick* did the late King of Prussia but thus "Thou great man Washington! what meaneth the bleeting of these black sheep and the lowing of these Negro oxen that till thy ground? Say not, they belong to thy wife; they are entailed to her relations as an inheritance. Such paltry excuses are beneath thy character."

The great defender of Liberty should give an example to his neighbors, worthy of himself. How much more honorable to pay wages and let them support themselves. Experience evinces even in this country, that it would be more profitable to the employer.

O God of Liberty! convince the world not only of the heinous sin of slaveholding but of its madness and impolicy. If justice does not demand the manumission of slaves, I defy any man to prove there is such a thing as moral rectitude.

If Mount Vernon was not the house of bondage to so many men, I would call it a little paradise. The mansion modest, the garden neat, the meandering of the Potomac—distant hills and extensive fields combine to render the prospect delightful and would present a happy retirement for one of the greatest men in the Universe.

From the President's Seat, I proceeded through Colchester (a little village on Ocoquan Creek) to Dumfries, a port town on Quanuco Creek, four miles above its junction with the Potomac. It contains about 230 scattered houses, but not a single place of worship; the Court House, however, is open to all denominations. I

---

*This silly man being introduced to the King of Prussia addressed him "Thou demi-God great Frederick," to which the King replied, "Thou great fool little Dederick get out of my sight!"

reasoned with the people from the seat of the judge, of righteousness, temperance and judgment to come. It seems several of them could not stand the test, for they walked out before I finished my short discourse. This is not an uncommon custom in some parts of America, for many of the present inhabitants, according to Dr. Franklyn, are not quite so mannerly as their ancestors, the Indians. This may be owing in a great measure to the carelessness of ministers to speak common sense ; too many content themselves with mere declamation and threatening without ever attempting to enlighten the understanding.

In this neighborhood there are some pleasant spots, and many of the inhabitants mourning like just Lot for the iniquity of the city.

I passed through Falmouth, a little tobacco town containing about 140 dwellings, to Fredericksburg, a post town on the Rappahanock River, about 100 miles by land from its entrance into the Chesapeak. It carries on a brisk trade with the Atlantic towns and exports tobacco for Europe ; it has one Episcopalian church, and as they inform me, very little religion; it is 206 miles southwest of Philadelphia, and 69 from Richmond, the seat of government for Virginia.

On my route towards Richmond I passed over a considerable extent of fine level country, interspersed with pretty houses and good taverns with excellent accommodations. It is observable that in these states the offices of driving and holding the plough devolve upon one person and are commonly performed by the negro girls.

The first thing that attracts the attention of the traveller at Richmond is an elegant capitol, with magnificent pillars supporting a lofty portico, and forming a prominent prospect in the city from the town of Manchester, the other side of James river. The bridge over it is about 400 yards in length, connecting the town and city together. It is situated at the foot of the falls by which a canal is now cutting that when completed will render the river navigable 460 miles from the Chesapeak. The coal pits in the vicinity are expected to furnish a great part of the Union with that valuable article. They are already worked to great advantage. Ten years ago this place could not boast of above 50 houses, but it now contains upwards of 1000.

On Sunday in the afternoon I was invited to preach in the house of representatives and most of the members attended.

The Virginians have done much towards abolishing the feudal system from their commonwealth, but some of its remains are still apparent. Lands are sacred, they cannot be sold to recover just debts. Glebes are still in the possession of Episcopal clergy, and the human species are transferred as chattels from father to son. "These things should not be so." Most of the State Legislators, who are at present in Assembly, acknowledge this slur on their character and blush that they have it not in their power to apply an immediate remedy. How difficult it is for slave holders to enter into the Kingdom of Heaven! O America, be ready to meet thy God. He hath prepared his bow and whetted His sword; His arrows fly fast in Europe, and His sword is bathed in blood in the West Indies. He will soon visit this continent unless thou wilt let the Africans go free. Proclaim then the acceptable year that it may no longer be said "This is a Land of Liberty full of Slaves."

From the general character of the Virginian's being free, friendly and volatile it may be expected that it will not be long ere they perform this just and generous act. God of love! grant it may be this year, lest the next should be too late—lest the Blacks in their turn should measure to the Whites as it was meted to them. Should this be the case, the latter can have no just reason to complain. May the present Legislators abolish every bad law and enact new ones so intelligible as not to need a lawyer to explain them, and so good as to preclude the necessity of a magistrate to assist Rebellion.

I am sorry the English mode of canvassing at elections is not altogether banished from this land. It is astonishing that the feelings of men in a free country should ever permit them to put up for public offices and solicit the votes of their fellow citizens! Had I ten thousands voices, I would never give one of them to a candidate who intreated for my interest. Let the citizens seek their own servants and enquire into their merits before they choose them to office. Let them be elected if possible without their knowledge of the appointment.

After crossing James river at Richmond I rambled through the country. Many of the inhabitants are decently clad in their own manufactures. They have some good farms. The soil is sandy, unless it be on the banks of rivers and creeks where it is black and rich. The best wheat I have seen this year is in the neighborhood of Petersburg, a trading town on the Appomattox river. Warehouses for tobacco, stores and a valuable mill are the most noted things in it. The inhabitants which amount to about 3,000 are subject to Fall fevers. The situation of the town is low and pleasantly surrounded with hills.

From Petersburg I followed the Post road to Hicks Ford (forty-five miles) on both sides of which the country is thickly populated. But it is a general custom in this State to build houses at some distance from the roads which renders it very disagreeable to a man when he loses his way which a stranger must be liable to very often for want of directing posts.

The principal productions of Virginia are tobacco, wheat, oats, persimmons, peaches, chincapink and all manner of fruit; fine saddle horses, plenty of partridges and other game. Lands in general are cheaper than to the northward. Abundance may be bought from one dollar to ten per acre, with improvements.

The first town I came to after entering North Carolina was Halifax, situated on the west side of Roanoke River. It is esteemed unhealthy. The inhabitants have erected a place of worship, free to every sect who believe in the existence of God ; some thought it ought to be on a more liberal scale, that atheists, if there were such beings, might have an equal chance with others in supporting their doctrine. It was accordingly voted to be open to all. Truth requires no more. A free investigation of every subject will lead the mind to the desired object. Infidelity must spread until superstition is destroyed ; then and not till then rational religion will prevail over the world.

On my journey from Halifax to Raleigh, the metropolis of North Carolina, I was accompanied by one of the delegates, who gave me much information respecting the country. State lands may be purchased at about $3.00 per hundred acres, but for this century it is probable a great part of them will not be worth one dollar per hundred. However, our honest speculators will sell the sandy and pine barrens, where you may trace the foot of a turkey, for second and first-rate lands, if they can meet with any so simple as to believe them. You had better beware of such people on your side of the water, as they have agents in every part of Europe.

Although liberty has been fostered in this State since the Revolution, the law will not permit a man to liberate his own slaves except in extraordinary cases ; this is tying the devil to one's back with a witness ; I should rather he would go to the numerous herds of swine which we daily meet on the roads going to the Virginia markets. Some of the wealthy farmers in this country drive five or six hundred hogs to market at a time—all of their own rearing, and weighing on an average from one to two cwt. Pork sells this year from $4 to $5 per cwt. This is certainly an excellent country for hog and hominy, and a traveler ought to accustom himself to live upon them, although other provisions may be procured at most of the inns.

Gentlemen in these parts are very hospitable, and esteem it a favor when strangers well recommended call upon them. The country is varigated with some good spots of land ; the timber, mostly pine and oak. On the last day of the year 1794 I crossed the Tar and New Rivers to Raleigh, where with your permission I shall conclude my long letter. Yesterday we were weather-bound and this day has been for the most part wet ; as yet I have had no winter, and so great a proportion of fine weather I never experienced in the Old World. May wind and waves be propitious to the friends of freedom on their passage to the New. Dear brother, farewell'

Yours, &c.   M. J. R.

Raleigh, North Carolina, January 1st, 1795.

(Letter 7th.)

Georgetown, S. C., January 12th, 1795.

Having finished my last letter at the seat of government for North Carolina, I shall now give you a short description of it. The situation is inland near the centre of the State, 25 miles from the nearest navigable water; the spot is level and deemed healthy, and may very well suit the purposes of legislation. Commercial towns are not always the best adapted for the residence of Legislators. In such places they are perhaps apt to attend to their own avocations to the neglect of public duty. In large towns and cities gambling houses are likewise sources of corruption and immorality. Were it proper to establish any test as a qualification for office, gamblers and dissipated characters ought to be deprived of that honor. Experience has sufficiently proved that such persons are not to be relied on in the hour of temptation. Is it probable that men who cannot regulate their own conduct or govern their passions, should properly legislate and rule others ?

In the evening of the first day of the year I was invited to speak in the House of Representatives. The members formed the principal part of my audience. I addressed them on the subjects of liberty, fraternity and signs of the times. Even here we find many who hail the happy day of emancipation, whilst others tremble at the idea of letting their negroes go free.

As I promised to give you a short account of customs and manners, I cannot help relating to you what happened at the close of the last mentioned discourse. When the people were about to disperse the Speaker of the House addressed them in a few words, hoping they would not forget their travelling friend who had come from a far country to visit them. Immediately hats were held up and money thrown into them. In vain I told my friends that I did not go about to preach for lucre—they thought, however, that ministers could not travel without money. I thanked them for their politeness, and spent the evening very agreeably with many of the members. They have as yet but scanty accommodation—every house is full. Two years ago there was not a mansion in the place. At present, including log houses, it contains about a hundred. The Capitol or State House is large and convenient.

On the second day I left Raleigh and posted over several creeks and one river (Cape Fear) by several huts, but very few decent houses, and still more miserable soil—a few spots excepted. We travelled forty-five miles and our entertainment was but indifferent. At night we put up at a little tavern where we were charged an exorbitant price for fodder.

Next morning we breakfasted at Fayetteville, on Cape Fear river. This is reckoned the greatest trading town in N. C. It has been named after the unfortunate La Fayette, of France, who after defending the dearest rights of the Americans, and commencing a glorious revolution in his own country, split his bark on the rock of royalty, and now suffers abundantly more under royal despots than if he had died through the instrumentality of the Robespierrian party.

Fayetteville being no longer the seat of government, buildings, etc., appear to be at a stand. The court house is their only place of worship—open to all. We proceeded on our journey to Lumberton. A great number of the settlers along this road are Scotchmen and their descendants. The little labor necessary for their support is performed without the aid of Negroes. What then becomes of the objection? "This country cannot be cultivated without slaves." Surely the soil that cannot be cultivated by the hands of freemen, ought for ever to remain a Wilderness.

Powell's tavern and Willis' store appear to be the main pillars of Lumberton, which is situated on Drowning river, navigable for barges from thence to George town. We had preaching at the Court House on Sunday, and visited a friend in the evening who lives comfortably on a farm of about 2000 acres, but not above forty cleared. Nevertheless he procures plenty of cotton and wool to make cloths; beef, pork, poultry, butter, cheese and bread to eat; cider, wine and brandy to drink—the produce of his own plantation. This good man (a blacksmith) has likewise erected a meeting house on his land. If there be no preachers he gives a word of exhortation to the people himself. Everyone who understands the gospel has a right and ought according to his abilities to preach it.

Being about to quit North Carolina, I shall just observe that although this climate approximates that of Spain, as yet there are not many sheep folds ; the wolves, they say, are not totally destroyed and the bears do some mischief. Manufactures in every State will perhaps flourish first far from the sea, and surely sheep will thrive better on the high lands sweetened with lime-stone than on these sandy bottoms.

We entered South Carolina at Barfield's Mills, where we crossed the Little Pedee and were glad to have a night's residence in a house consisting of one long room, where the rich and the poor meet together, to eat, sleep, work and worship. The proprietor appears to be a public spirited man, but like too many of that excellent stamp, has not been successfull in all his schemes. "Count the cost" is the maxim of the prudent ; it is easy to project beyond the ability to perform.

Next morning we could not travel far, owing to a heavy fall of rain ; when we had turned to a house for shelter, the landlord insisted on sending three or four miles round for his neighbors, to hear what a stranger had to say to them ; the people were attentive, but there is an Achan in the camp, and until that is destroyed there can be no genuine success. I have not missed an opportunity from New York here of administering as many abolition pills as I thought could be well digested.

In the evening we travelled 'till a dark night overtook us, when we missed our way in the woods and imagined we should be out all night. Had I believed the doctrine of ghosts and hobgoblins, should have readily conceived that they were our conductors at this time. At length, however, we found a friend's house, a descendant of the ancient Britons. Higher up on the Pedee is a place called Welsh Neck, originally settled by Welsh Cambrians.

Another wet morning. But we have not had six days that could be called humid, since the 12th of October. Last summer, however, it is said the inundations were so great in this part, that the produce on the low grounds was totally destroyed. The deluge must be great indeed to supplant that valuable grain called Indian corn. The stalk is so strong and the ear so fortified with the husk, that nothing short of a flood or violent storm can injure it. The more I am acquainted with its qualities, the more I admire its virtues. Thousands of negroes exist upon it—at least it is their principal support in this country. Some families allow them the addition of salt, and others a portion of beef once a year on Christmas. This must be understood as advertising to what are called field or plantation Negroes, as those who are employed in houses live better than many hired servants in Europe. Indian corn to those who are accustomed with it both in bread and hominy is excellent food. I know of no grain, so generally useful for the support of man and beast. It fattens all kinds of cattle, horses, hogs and poultry, and the blades may be classed with the best of fodder. I am sorry we are now come to a part of the country where rice-straw is given to the horses as a miserable substitute.

This day we had to pass through several savannas or swampy meadows, and owing to a flood in the great Pedee 'twas with great difficulty we could ferry over. We passed by a few good plantations, and after crossing Lynch's Creek, put up at Davies' tavern (a Cambro Briton married a French woman) where we were very well entertained Sans depense.

There is generally a sameness in the surface of this country. We met nothing particularly worth describing in the road, unless it being so uniform and level, that the sight was often lost between lofty rows of pine waving their evergreen heads with the gentle breezes.

After crossing Black River, at Evans' Ferry, we arrived at George-Town to dinner at the house of another Cymro from Bala—the only tavern in the town, which consists of 150 houses. Its low situation and the numerous rice plantations in its vicinity are circumstances very much against its health and prosperity. It has no immediate trade with Europe, although it lies within fourteen miles of the ocean at the junction of the Pedee, the Black and Sampit rivers. Previous to the American War it had immediate communications with England, but during that period the British and Tories burnt the greater part of the town and the depredations everywhere in this country was worthy of their infamous cause. A French privateer has just brought in a Spanish letter of marque ; the crew of the former are filled with enthusiasm ; victory or death seems to pervade the soul of every Frenchman ; they sing, fight and conquer. I wish they may go on until they break the shackles of 'slavery from the feet of the oppressed in all lands and nations. Is it possible that an old stale British law should still exist in this State to prohibit under £100 penalty the instruction of Negroes?

Sorry am I to say that the white people in the Southern States are initiated from their infancy into a system of barbarous cruelty; even the most beautiful, delicate and in other respects amiable ladies, who can hardly stoop to pick up a handkerchief or move a chair, will handle a cow-skin to flog their slaves with amazing dexterity. But the Negroes, they say, will not work without flagellation. Some of them, it's true, have such an exalted sense of freedom that they will suffer the flesh to be torn off their backs rather than submit to their tyrants; others are remarkable for their obedience and gratitude to those who use them generously.

I must bid you adieu. The South Carolinans, as far as I have seen of them, are polite and friendly to strangers, but every species of civility that does not embrace the distressed of every clime is in my opinion of the mulish kind, which only serves the vanity or interest of the possessor. M. J. R.

(Letter 8th.)

CHARLESTON, January 24, 1795.

None but those who die in infancy quit the world as they find it; good or evil is left behind by all who traverse this globe, transient must the stay of travellers be not to communicate vice or virtue. Whilst at Georgetown the opportunities were frequent to impress the latter on the minds of the inhabitants, nor were my pleasures confined to imparting, I enjoyed real felicity in receiving instructions from the lips of intelligent friends. One of them accompanied us to this place. But as usual I must give you a short view of our route, the most remarkable part of it was the curious navigation of the Push-and-go creek, down which meandering stream we had to go 4 miles before we crossed the Santee river. This creek was well named for we were constantly tacking about and often entangled in the branches of the trees. In the evening our friend took us to a squire's house near the road, the family being absent we could find no white man on the plantation excepting the slave driver. After supper we conversed with the negroes, many of whom had a thirst after knowledge and sang well. They entertained us with roasted potatoes, which was the only article they could spare.

Next morning we arrived opposite this town to breakfast, (28 miles). The road was excellent. We passed by three or four Episcopalian places of worship quite forsaken and desolate, "no penny no pater noster." The country has, however, more preachers than the people are perhaps willing to hear, especially if they preach against slavery.

After crossing the bay, which is about three miles over, we saluted our friends in the capital of the Southern States. The citizens are sociable and friendly, many of them intelligent and communicative. The description they have given me of some plantations is truly dreadful. Negroes not only half naked, but totally uncovered penned up at night and awoke each morning by the music of whips which are so often applied to their backs that there is scarcely an inch without a scar or a wound. If some of the most knowing of the slaves take upon them to instruct and console their comrades the most barbarous treatment takes place to tantalize them to silence. If every other method fails the bablers are sold and banished from their friends in order to get rid of their impertinences, but it is too late, the seed is sown and the little leaven of liberty, which is now hid from the eyes of many, will soon leaven the whole lump of mankind.

The orphan house in Charleston I visited with pleasure. It is a noble institution for white children, but the black negroes being of an inferior order, cannot be admitted. The city library has a good shell where many valuable books may be deposited. The collection is already tolerable, admitting its infantile state; I hope every deposit for useful knowledge will be enlarged until the torch of truth has illumined the earth.

I happened to enter the goal at a time when it had not a single prisoner; during that period two were sent in, one for manslaughter and the other for vending bills knowing them to be forged. The criminal laws in this state have not yet undergone the necessary reformation. They have, however, a merciful judge. Lately whilst addressing a criminal who was to be executed he administered consolation by assuring him "that they should all soon follow in the same way." To another he said "tomorrow you must be hanged by the neck till you die, and the Lord have mercy on your soul between 12 and 1 o'clock." I need not inform you what countryman this gentleman is, nor have I mentioned the above by way of reflection on the judge, for (a few such innocent blunders excepted) he is one of the most intelligent and amiable of men.

I will not pretend to give you a particular description of Charleston. Its plan is regular, with parallel streets running from Ashley to Cooper river. These are intersected at right angles, but most of them are too narrow for this climate. The old houses are built chiefly of wood, of late brick prevails and some of the dwellings are neat and well furnished for the summer season with piazzas and balconies. Although the town is not more than seven feet above the surface of the water, they say it is healthy to those who constantly reside in it, but it often proves fatal to strangers who may arrive in the summer and fall. Many of the inhabitants migrate at that period to the northward and to the islands in its vicinity.

The commerce of Charleston is considerable with Europe and the West Indies The exports of last year amounted to $3,846,392. It contained, according to the census of 1790, 16,400 inhabitants, of whom 7,700 were slaves. The population of the state, according to the returns in 1791, is 141,979 free persons and 107,094 slaves. Near the sea coast the negroes are the most numerous. The legislature has wisely prohibited any further importation from Africa.

The staple commodity of this part is rice; indigo, cotton, tobacco, tar, pitch, turpentine and lumber are likewise exported in great quantities. One of the principal improvements in this state is a canal now cutting to form a communication between the Santee and Cooper rivers. The adventurers, it is said, are likely to be losers for some time.

There are several colleges and academies in South Carolina and literature has been considerably encouraged since the Revolution, nevertheless many young gentlemen are sent to the Eastern states to finish their education.

Although religion profited more than anything else by the separation of the United States from Britain, having no test or establishment to retard its progress, yet on account of the distinction kept up between white and black there are barriers against its promulgation and considerable difficulties opposed to its success. In Charleston the sects are as numerous as in most towns and their clergy well supported by voluntary contributions. Whilst on the subject of religion it may not be amiss to notice the devotion of the French on the 21st of January, whilst commemorating the death of Louis XVI. In the morning of this day they had a grand procession through the streets. An altar of liberty was erected a little out of town on Bocquet's Green, where an excellent band of music performed. The orator appointed for the day addressed the audience on the occasion and the oath of eternal hatred to tyrants was solemnly administered with uplifted hands. Several hymns and odes to liberty were sung. A short prayer imploring the divine aid in behalf of the French nation and the emancipation of all mankind concluded the ceremony. After this shouts of "Vive la Republique" bursted the air and penetrated the portals of heaven. The memory of the man who was once idolized is now (as all idols ought to be) despised and execrated.   M. J. K.

(Letter 9th.)

SAVANNAH, February 4th, 1795.

If in theory we are obliged to admit the doctrine of free agency, experience daily evinces that it is not altogether in man to direct his steps. We are not always governed even by motives, for stern necessity often prevents us from choosing our lot. A future state of retribution sufficiently demonstrates the truth of moral ability and both nature and revelation prove the fact of philosophical necessity—where then shall we draw the line? How shall we reconcile apparent difficulties? O the depth of the wisdom of God! Let us rest satisfied with the declaration of Jesus—"you shall know hereafter."

Ten years have elapsed since I took my passage from London to Charleston. I was upon the point of sailing when an unforseen event changed my course—a second attempt from Bristol proved abortive. This led me seriously to contemplate the Divine Government, and I trust the reflections will never be erased from my mind. Had Providence then permitted me to cross the ocean, I should not have borne my testimony against many bad laws and iniquitous practises in my native country, nor perhaps have drank so deep of the cup of manumission. Having stood on the ruins of the Bastile at Paris and still feeling the energy of those principles which shake Europe to the centre, I am now constrained to preach Liberty to captives, and proclaim the acceptable year of the Lord.

Judging of your feelings by my own, I shall avoid egotism as much as possible, but as a traveller, I find it impracticable not to exhibit something of myself in the picture I present you. Although I tarried at Charleston but twelve days it was time to depart, else attachment to friends might have made parting more difficult— more cordial companions could not have been met with; two of them accompanied us ten and a half miles out of town—where at our parting dinner we had a concert of frogs to entertain us in lieu of more excellent musicians. It is astonishing what a clatter those little animals make in this part of the country. Its swampy bottoms are fine nurseries for them, nor is game and wild fowl less plentiful. Hundreds of ducks and geese are constantly seen and may be easily approached almost every where as we travel along the road.

The first night after we left Charleston our lodgings were at Judge Bxx's, an active citizen at the time of the Revolution, and who I believe continues to deserve well of his country. I wish his sentiments upon the diabolical practice of duelling were not only known but adopted by every government. They are short and in my opinion would be more decisive than the Prussian ordinance of punishing with death. Let the challenger and acceptor be forever deprived of the privileges of citizens. The thoughts of being cashiered and incapacitated for holding any office of honor or emolument would perhaps act as a strong sedative on the minds of the would-be courageous. The brave are above being revengeful nor will the truly noble suffer their dignity to be disgraced by permitting a contemptible Coxcomb to rob him of life.

We crossed the Edistow River, at Jacksonburgh, and owing to the freshets 'twas with difficulty we could wade through some creeks, particularly at Fish Pond and Saltcatchers. In the evening to Coosawhatchie, where I had to lecture in the Court House, the gentleman who entertained us told me that he came to this country at the close of the war without hat, cap, shirt or shoes that were worth wearing. He possesses now about 5000 acres of land, fine houses and plenty of Negroes. The wheels of Providence are ever guided by the God of love. But ungrateful men abuse his blessing, when they rivet on others the fetters which fell from their own feet.

From Coosawhatchie we steered our course for Col. S—— on May River, from whence we came in a canoe to this place (distance about thirty miles). The meandering of this stream, the oyster shoals, pomadum trees, etc., on its banks were truly agreeable scenes, but when we had entered the Savannah River, the wind having risen we were likely to be overwhelmed by its waves. However, we arrived safe at the desired haven and had occasion to "Praise the Lord for His goodness and his wonderful works to the children of men."

At Savannah I have already met with several gentlemen whose urbanity cannot be excelled. What surprises me, they boast of the salubrity of their situation and adduce as proof the longevity of the inhabitants. The city stands on an elevated bluff and every breeze of wind causes a shower of sand, which salutes the tyrant as well as the slave with a "How do you do Brother Dust?" The plan of the town is oblong, abounding with squares, which furnishes a free communication of air to every street. The exports of last year amounted to $263,830. The great descent from the bluff to the river is a considerable obstruction to its trade, particularly in the summer, when the reflection of heat from the sand on the surface of the water becomes intense and proves mortal to many.

One day in company with a party of friends I took an excursion to see Whitfield's Orphan House. Nothing but the shattered wings remain, in which we found some broken screen maps, a whole length painting of the late Countess of Huntingdon, and a poor family. It is beyond the stretch of my imagination to comprehend what could induce the good man to fix upon so barren a spot for such a purpose; but no reflection on the dead. His intentions were no doubt good, although he miserably misapplied the donations of the public in purchasing slaves to support orphans and students in divinity. "Providence frowned on the deed, and a flash of lightning (as is supposed) burnt the college and chapel to the ground. Lady H. repaired the wings and sent over several young men to be here qualified for the ministry; most of them have since joined the Baptist and Presbyterians. The last tutor was the intrepid Johnson, who after the death of Lady H. was forced to quit possession of the premises. By a certain clause in Mr. Whitfield's will the property became disputable; the State of Georgia interfered and terminated the affair by decreeing that the whole should be placed under the inspection of commissioners, who are to apply the property to its primitive object. As yet they have done nothing except banishing the courageous J, who would not quit his mansion till he was taken Vi et Armis! On our return we visited the plantation where he lived; it had been purchased, with the slaves thereon, by Mr. W. to establish a revenue for the maintenance of the orphans, &c. What pleased me most in this ramble was the beautiful varigation of shrubbery and trees, most of which in this climate are clad with a never-fading vendure. The fan pomadum and the myrtle are favorites of the soil; from the berries of the latter, with the addition of a little wax, are made excellent candles. The bay trees are of a larger growth than I ever saw. The sour orange, the peach and the lime bestow their fruit in great abundance, and are lovely appendages to a sultry situation. The kitchen garden through the winter is in its prime, and the cattle in the country during that period have occasion for little or no dry fodder.

There are but few nations that can boast of such advantageous variations as the United States. They produce within their own limits all the necessaries and luxuries of life. No part of the globe is better adapted for independence, and could a Chinese policy be adopted as it regards imported articles (without prohibiting the migration of mechanics into it from other countries), it would soon, like that empire, become invincible in itself. But you are ready to retort, because the propagation of such principles ill becomes a citizen of the world, granted—and another word shall not be said in its defence. The rage for every thing foreign is sufficient to make us suspicious of the patriotism of some characters. For my own part, I always feel a propensity for living on and wearing the productions of the country wherein I reside. Notwithstanding this propendency, I would have commerce be as free as air, un-shackled by treaties and disencumbered as much as possible from customs. If the love of our country be a cardinal virtue, every nation ought to have as great a proportion of it as to prefer its own manufactures to those of others. The prevalence of this principle would preclude the necessity of heavy imports by way of encouraging our own artists. As for its being a good method of raising a revenue, I have only to say that the mystery of just taxation has not been revealed, at least it has not been generally practised, for every system that does not equalize the tax upon property whether visible or invisible must be iniquitous because unjust. It no doubt requires wisdom and magnanimity in legislators to devise and execute such a plan, but the difficulties attending it are by no means insurmountable.

Excuse this digression. Having dined with an honest lawyer in company with many more of the cloth, I was led to the above disquisition. The worthy and eloquent pleader I refer to, is noted for advocating the cause of the poor and distressed. Last week and old woman came to him, imploring his aid in behalf of her son, then in prison. He enquired for what crime he had been put there? She answered: "for galloping sir." (They have a law in Savannah against galloping in the streets). "But did he gallop over any person?" "No sir!" "Where then did he gallop?" "Only about thirty-six miles out of town sir." "Then I presume he stole the horse?" "Indeed, indeed he only galloped away with him, sir." Such gallopers are too common in America as well as Europe.

(Letter 10th.)

SAVANNAH, February 21, 1795.

DEAR FRIEND:—And must I again bear testimony against the worst of crimes and alas once more relate the tale of woe because of oppression my heart is grieved, and in beholding the sufferings of the oppressed my soul is deluged with sorrow. Surely the iniquity of Georgia is near it's zenith, for in defiance of the most powerful convictions she continues to carry on the trade of blood and bind with chains the innocent victims of her avarice. It is the only state in the Union whose ports are open to enslave the poor kidnapped African, but to their shame be it spoken, there are too many merchants from Maine to St. Mary engaged in the barbarous traffic.

Lately in this city several negroes were taken up and publicly flogged for assembling together to worship God. They began with their preacher, who said with a smile, that if it suited their purpose best they might even kill him. Refusing to be tried, he stood and bore without a sigh, the scorpion lash. The rest followed his example and with uplifted hands to heaven appeared emulous who should receive the first stroke. Foolish Pharoahs! Know ye not that the more ye persecute the more Israel will increase?

It would take up a volume to relate the excesses of some task masters. They have no compassion even upon pregnant women, but drive them unmercifully to the moment of delivery. Some are tortured to death for not accomplishing a task which nature could never perform. Such as have more merciful masters and are well clad are liable to be killed if they go from home without protection. An instance lately occurred of a negro who being decently dressed was taken up by a malicious driver, had his clothes torn from him and actually flogged to death for daring to appear in such apparel. A wretch in this neighborhood, after shooting a negro dead from mere wantonness, boasts of the deed. The patience of Jehovah is verily great, otherwise he would consume such vermin from the creation.

To counteract the vice of slavery I have proposed to the friends of freedom the establishment of schools to teach the children of free negroes and others who may be permitted by their holders to receive instruction. Although many are anxious to see such a plan executed, yet, owing to their timidity and prudential reasonings, I am fearful of its success.

The black people here being prevented from assembling together to worship, unless a white man preached to them, I have endeavored to obviate this objection and the following petition will give you an idea of what has been done:

To the friends of humanity and religion the following case is presented by a Christian church, consisting of the people of color, living in Savannah and its vicinity:

We were formed into a regular church in the year 1788; Andrew Bryan, a black man, was appointed pastor, under whose ministry many have received convictions of sin and have proved their sincerity by a visible change of conversation and conduct. We pretend not to have a perfect church, but considering our unfriendly circumstances, few have disgraced their profession. When any are found to walk disorderly they have no longer fellowship with us till by consistent conduct the sincerity of their repentance is manifested. Nevertheless, we have been deprived of the free gift of God to every rational creature.

The absence of that civil liberty which is by white men so much valued, we must, it seems, as Christians patiently endure; but to be deprived of the inestimable privilege of peaceably assembling in our own meeting house, to worship Jehovah, is an affliction insupportably grievous.

Formerly when we convened, for mutual worship, the cruel lash inflicted the body till the blood streamed down our backs. That severity has partly subsided. It is, however, succeeded by a distressing delay of the long desired blessing.

We have repeatedly petitioned the magistrates, but the following is the only grant we could obtain:

CITY COUNCIL, December 24, 1794.

A petition from the people of color, praying to have liberty to worship Almighty God was received and read, and as the said petition is supported by a respectable number of citizens, it is ordered that they be at liberty to assemble on Sunday, the 4th day of January, 1795. That the said meetings shall commence after 10 o'clock in the forenoon and disperse before 4 o'clock in the afternoon of each day. Extract from the minutes. WILLIAM NORMENT, Clerk.

Alas! in the land of liberty our toleration to worship God is limited to two days, and only twelve hours in the year, and for aught we know, forever. Where shall we turn our eyes? There is no place of worship in the city open nor convenient to receive us. Peaceable in the neighborhood and obedient to our masters, must we be deprived of the chief consolation we had in this life? Oh fellow men, fellow Christians, think of our condition and afford us your friendly aid! Though the color of our skin differ from yours, we have the same claim on humanity, the same hope of immortal blessedness.

Our only petition at present is to have the privilege of worshipping God in the assembly of his saints.

Signed in behalf of about four hundred members and near four hundred more who wish to be baptised, but have not as yet obtained leave by their masters, by
ANDREW BRYAN, Pastor.

SAMPSON BRYAN, } Deacons.
EVAN CLAY, }

'We, the subscribers, having considered the above case, think that the best means of relieving our brethren of color is the erecting of a place of worship, large and convenient, to hold both black and white people together. The principal objection being against the latter to assemble alone. We have, therefore, entered into a contract to build such a place in the city of Savannah, 60x50 feet, with galleries all round. We have subscribed among ourselves in Savannah about 400 pounds sterling, but the building, before it is finished, will cost about 1000 pounds sterling. We trust that the friends of religion and liberty, throughout the Union, will join us in assisting those who are deprived of the means of assisting themselves.

EBENEZER HILLS,
JOHN HAMILTON,
THOMAS HARRISON, } Citizens of Savannah.
JOHN H. ROBERTS,
JOHN MILLEN, etc.

Savannah, Georgia, February 24, 1795.

Having been requested to give this new meeting house a name, considering present circumstances I know of no better title than the house of peace, accordingly it is to be called Beth-Shallom. The constitution they have adopted will, I hope, procure the congregation the blessing as well as the name of peace. As it contains but four articles I will transcribe it.

1. Jesus Christ is the only head of the church.
2. Believers in him are the only members.
3. They are to choose their own officers.
4. The Bible is their only rule of faith and practice.

If the prejudice of the white people does not subside I have no doubt but the blacks will deport themselves with decorum. You would be surprised to see their good order and regularity at meetings, and as to singing their music is far superior to any I have yet heard on this continent.'

Before I close my letter I shall take a trip to Sunbury and Newport, 40 miles to the southward. I have been to the little Ogeechie, where the imagination or the pencil had little or nothing to describe. The peach begins to blossom and the birds warble their matrimonial notes, but like a sparrow on the housetop mourning after its mate, so do I lament the loss of a fellow traveller who accompanied me from Baltimore to this place. Truly two are better than one to sojourn in a strange land, but why should I complain.

"Since God is ever present, ever felt,
In the void waste as in the city full;
And where He vital breathes, there must be joy."

But now I proceed with the honest attorney to his country seat on the great Ogeechie. Over this river there is a tollerable drawbridge, but at the end of it we got fast in the mud and all hands were employed in getting the phaeton and horses out of the quag. Then we had for two miles a causeway, which might be properly called the perfection of bad roads. The attorney endeavored to show cause why the causeway was so miserable and promised it should be soon mended. In the afternoon we amused ourselves with shooting and had plenty of sport, game being everywhere abundant. Next morning being a day of general thanksgiving throughout the United States for providential mercies, we went to midway meeting house, where we had a good discourse on the occasion by the Rev. Mr. G. After about ½ an hour's rest I was requested to address the audience, which I did by endeavoring to rivet the nail that had been previously fixed. In this meeting all the white males were armed with pistols or muskets. The law obliges them to assemble in this manner partly on account of the Indians who now and then scout in the neighborhood; it likewise has a tendency to keep the negroes in awe, who here are by far the most numrouse. The midway settlement, although respectable and long established, is not congenial to the health of the white inhabitants, for they are constantly diminishing in number.

In the evening we arrived at Sunbury where we were well received by Dr. McQ., who presides over the academy. This little place has a spacious harbour and is agreeably situated at the head of St. Catharine's sound. It was burnt by the British in the last war and as yet has but few houses rebuilt. The commerce which formerly belonged to the port has been turned into a different channel. Although I was offered by a namesake at Sunbury a free passage to St. Mary's, (the extreme of the Union,) I could not accept it on account of previous engagements. We returned by Newport, an infant town full of business. The country affording no variety of picturesque views, our conversation was principally upon religion and politics. As we often dream at night of what occurred in the day, I am tempted in this place to present you with my vision on the night succeeding the Thanksgiving Day. My mind being fixed upon that part of the president's proclamation wherein he prays "and finally to impart all the blessings we possess or ask for ourselves to the whole family of mankind," nobly said, etc.

(Letter IIth.)

AUGUSTA, March 2nd, 1795.

DEAR FRIEND:—The visions of my head having led me to Mount Vernon, to behold the President of the United States manumitting his Negroes, the delicious entertainment tempted me to dream a second time. In my reveries I saw assembled in a magnificent temple dedicated to Liberty, all the Legislators and Ministers of Religion within the United States. A person of middle stature, whose countenance bespoke integrity and firmness, rose, and having fixed his eyes on the Legislators, thus addressed them:

CITIZENS:—You stand in the place of God, &c,

After a short but solemn pause, he turned to the Preachers of Xtianity (Christianity) and with an uplifted hand spake as follows:

MEN AND BRETHREN:—Your profession is honorable. You are, &c.

The company gazed at each other in silence; a consciousness of guilt was visible in their faces, but they dreaded the consequences of emancipating their brickmakers. At length the voice of Virtue resounded through the hall and instantly Righteousness was seated on the tribune; Vice made a feeble opposition by urging the imprudence of putting Justice at that period in the chair. The voice of Truth was however heard like the trumpet from Sinai, demanding audience, and finally proving that there never was or will be a period when Justice should not preside in that assembly.

A loud call for the question whether it was just to grant equal liberty to all men, whatever their complexion be, roused me out of sleep, and all I can recollect to have taken place in the interim was the reading of a Congressional Declaration of Rights, worded July 4th, 1776, as follows: "We hold these truths to be self-evident—that all men are created equal; that they are endowed by their Creator with certain unalienable rights; that among these are life, liberty and the pursuit of happiness; that to secure these rights governments are instituted among men, deriving their just power from the consent of the governed; and whenever any form of government becomes destructive to these ends, it is the right of the people to alter or to abolish it and to institute new government, laying its foundation on such principles, and organizing its powers in such form as to them shall seem most likely to effect their safety and happiness." Whether the United States would have the magnanimity to execute this decree and apply it universally, was not discovered to me. I have, however, hazarded an opinion in some letters which I have just wrote in answer to a pamphlet entitled Negro Slavery defended by the Word of God.

I now bid adieu to the melancholy subject and proceed on my journey to Kentucky and the N. W. Territory. In this route you must not expect to have a description of any thing like the Chef D'Ouvres and antiquities of Italy; the magnificent louvres of France; or the sublime neatness and uniformity of Holland; but if the Author of Nature will give me a pencil to paint His works, perhaps mountains, deserts and plains may make stranger and more durable if not finer impressions on your mind.

Just as I was about to quit Savannah, I received a polite letter (a copy of which I transmit to you) not out of vanity, but merely to show the liberal spirit of its author. Many of the citizens pressed hard upon me to return and reside among them, but it is vain to calculate on futurity ; we know not what a day will bring forth. Health being the most valuable of all earthly blessings, that manner of living which procures the greatest share of it, should be followed, and traveling has hitherto been my best physician ; but my friends portray the prospect of my present pilgrimage in dark and dismal colors. Its commencement has not turned out very pleasant, being seized the first night after I left Savannah with a violent influenza. The next day I tarried awhile at a Dutch settlement, of whose Minister the President of the United States said, "He is one of the most humble and modest men I ever saw." He showed me their meeting house which for this country is a very good one, but not too much so to be converted into a stable during the last war. I spent the evening with another clergyman who instead of fleecing his flock, had been sheared by them very closely.

Next day whilst waiting for dinner at a tavern the landlord questioned me about the meaning of all the difficult texts of Scripture he could think of, for which trouble I was entertained a la gallais. This person, to his praise be it spoken, was not more inquisitive in speech, than industrious about his dwelling. His little farm, although naturally barren, produces by skill and good management, excellent crops. The shading of summer follows with any kind of clover, beans, peas that may be turned up with the soil. It has proved of the greatest utility in most climates, but particularly the warm. This citizen manures his farm with a kind of weed natural to the soil. He sows the seed in the Spring and ploughs the whole up early in the Fall; thus instead of exposing his fallows to be destroyed by the Summer heat, he gains the advantage of manuring his land with its own productions.

Most things are purified by fire. Even the surface of the greater part of the pine barrens pass the ordeal once a year. What is called wire grass grows to a considerable height and must be burnt every Spring for the cattle seldom feed upon it after the first growth. This being the purifying season 'twas with difficulty I could get along in some places. The fire ran parallel vith, and often crossed the road, forming a kind of running blaze, which in one constant stream swept thousands of acres before it.

The further I traveled from the sea, the land grew better, but more broken, with many large ponds and meadows covered with water.

My influenza growing severe and an excellent horse which carried me all the way from New York being sick, I took my rest, the greater part of one day and night, with a member of the next Georgia Convention. Here I had the pleasure to see a large family engaged in husbandry and home manufactures ; the sons were employed in the field and the daughters in carding, spinning and weaving. The sight had a tendency to banish my disease, and Mrs. D. engaged to restore the health of my horse. She tied a piece of sassafras root in his mouth and let him stand for some time to chew it ; he was then sent into the wheat field to graze. It is common here to drive not only sheep but horses at this season to keep down the thriving wheat.

By next morning we were pretty well recovered and after refreshing ourselves at a very good inn on the road, we reached Augusta, where the first-rate land

114

commences and the trees, which indicate good soil, make their appearance; but bad as the pine lands are deemed to be, I have seen sufficient proofs of their being made very productive.

Where there is such an extent of territory and such a scope for speculation, it is natural for the inhabitants to be shifting and ever searching for the best spots.

The common topic of conversation for some time past has been concerning one of the greatest speculations and we may add peculations which ever took place in any country—about twenty-five millions of acres have been sold by the present Legislature for nearly a penny per acre, a great proportion of which is equal to any in the world. It is more than suspected that the majority of the members were bribed by the companies that purchased. The people are very clamorous against them and some have been obliged to fly; disputes and even wagers run high whether or not the laws can be repealed and the purchase be disannulled.*

Augusta is noted for speculators. It consists of about 200 houses mostly in one long level street on the banks of the Savannah River, which is navigable for barges a few miles higher up; from hence a considerable quantity ot tobacco, indigo and cotton is exported. The currents of this river are very much against importation, boats being sometimes three weeks coming up from Savannah here. They have now on the stocks a steam boat intended to sail against the stream; many attempts have been made, but as yet without effect, as the mechanism of the inventor has hitherto been too complex.

No discovery can be of greater utility to America than a simple method of rowing against the stream by means of engine or any other machine. Its immense inland navigation demands the exertions of every genius to find out this useful art. They talk of encouraging the liberal arts in this State, and keep much noise about religion but infidelty gains ground. A modern Theist lectures every Sunday morning in this town, simply on morality—Christianity is out of the question. Yesterday I heard a discourse in defence of revelation which would have been more useful and pleasing, but for its prolixity. Near the close several of the young bucks were unmannerly in the extreme. I thought of Robinson's prayer, "Lord forgive the impatience of the hearers and the tediousness of the speaker; through Jesus Christ our Lord, Amen."

The Episcopalian clergyman in whose pulpit I preached in the afternoon is truly a liberal man and a very excellent companion. He expressed an anxious desire to see an union of all denominations speedily taking place.

As I shall soon quit the Post road it may be a long while before you hear from me again. I shall endeavor to preserve my journal and perhaps copy it verbatim for your perusal. May the Governor of the universe guide, protect and bless you and yours with a full fruition of every felicity.   M. J. R.

(Letter 12.)

DEAR FRIEND:—Agreeable to promise, I transcribe my journal, in which you may find related some trifling affairs, whilst more essential articles are perhaps omitted. Having labored under considerable debility of body and mind and no Amanuensis

---

*This has been since done. The succeeding Legislature repealed the law, and had a grand procession to burn all the papers and records relative thereto in one conflagration.

to note down the occurences of the moment, my memory could not always recall the ideas and impressions which local circumstances made on my mind.

March 3rd. Left Augusta; breakfasted at Judge W————n's; Parson B. and his servant accompanied me as far as Bedford, a little village five or six miles from A. I have not seen many black coats so free from Buckram. How seldom do we meet with dignity of deportment; ease and amiability of manners in the same person! Feeling sick and distressed for want of a fellow-traveller, I halted early in the evening at the hospitable Col. S————s, who detained me over night and diverted me with Indian and Revolutionary tales in which he was well versed; he assured me that many of the Indian warriors were men of integrity, and by no means devoid of humanity.

4th. My intended route being over the mountains, I thought best to change my big horse for Col. S——'s little mare valued at £25 sterling. The roads begin to be rough and stoney; you may judge of those I have already traveled when I inform you that my horse had been rode from Vermont to Augusta (upwards to 1500 miles) with the same shoes. This day I rode but a few miles, having to preach in the evening at Elder M——'s.

5th. Started early and breakfasted at Ray's Mills; tolerable soil, but the surface, on account of its being so varigated, is liable to be washed by heavy rains. Dined at F. G., Esq., who is so exasperated against land speculators that he can scarcely forbear cursing them for the disgrace they have brought on their country. In the evening to Mr. S., where I met a gentleman just come from Kentucky, whither a great many are about moving from this neighborhood, some in quest of health, others to gratify a passion which amounts to a species of mania for migrating to the Westward.

6th. Passed through a little town called Washington; I went to see a mineral spring in its vicinity, to which Morse and others attribute many virtues. At present it is not much resorted to, nor do its qualities at this season appear to me extraordinary. In the evening to E. B., Esq.; nothing particular occurred, but the old tale of condemning the last Legislature. It is well for this country that it has so many virtuous characters.

7th. Went with Mr. B. to S. M.'s meeting house. The church held a conference and I was very much pleased with their deliberations on some important points of discipline. Their government is purely republican. Those who would find monarchy or aristocracy in the Gospel may as well expect fire in water or men growing like mushrooms out of the earth.

8th. Two sermons in the morning; the weather was cold and the people chilly; whenever I see a starving congregation, I think of "I will have mercy and not sacrifices;" some would have preached three or four hours from "Speak my words whether they hear or not;" returned in the evening with Mr. B. and exhorted at his house; the people attend with a degree of avidity, that shows they are anxious to understand.

9th. To Major L.'s, where I met Col. H. k., with whom I went home—of this man one of the members of Congress told me "He is a jewel of estimable value." In the course of our conversation this evening he has convinced me that few men possess more knowledge and merit, and yet he has never been elected by the Georgians to any office of honor or emolument.

10th. Mr. H., who is well acquainted with this country, informs me that the climate is congenial to all manner of fruit provided the planters understand its culture; excellent soil for barley, but the weavel and rust destroy the wheat; Indian corn and oats likewise thrive well—they may be bought now for 1 per bushel; cattle proportionately cheap; men may live well here provided they have health and that blessing with proper precaution may be obtained in as great a degree in this, as any other State; a bad practice prevails in most places of cutting down the trees which should shade the houses, where they don't grow naturally the weeping-willow, &c., ought to be planted as a preservative from the noxious exhalations of ponds and rotten trees; dined at the Rev. Mr. S———r's, part of whose congregation wanted to expell him for adopting Watts's Psalms in lieu of the old Scotch version; in the evening to Elder W., who with four or five other preachers with many of their neighbors are about starting to Kentucky, in consequence lands have fallen in price—good farms with considerable improvements may be bought for two dollars per acre.

11th. Spent the greatest part of this day in reading the history of this Western Territories; the empire of the earth has been for some time travelling towards the setting sun.

12th. Weather bound.

13th. To Elder S., who is about taking his numerous family over the Ohio, in order to be totally freed from the curse of Negro slavery; violent toothache; 'twas the reflection of a rake once, and the means of his conversion. If one little bone aches so much, what excruciating pain must the wicked feel when every joint will be tortured by Divine vengeance.

14th. Passed by Greaver's Mountain, which is supposed to contain iron, copper, gold and silver ore. The proprietor, an old English gentleman, thinks its value equal to all the State. On the road I was invited to address a company of citizens who had assembled to sign their acceptance of a small pittance of western land allotted them by the late infamous and shameless Assembly. Dastardly conduct! They ought to have treated the perjurors as traitors to their country. In company with Elder S. to Mr. W———e's between two and three hundred miles from the sea on the banks of the Savannah.

15th. To W———e's meeting house and after service to T———s's; very much fatigued. The rest of the laborer is sweet.

16th. Crossed the Savannah at Barksdale Ferry, where I met several families with their wagons moving from N. Carolina to Georgia, from whence many of the good folks are migrating as fast as they can. Wonderful country! whose inhabitants, like the waves of the sea, are constantly ebbing and flowing East, West, North and South. Here I entered South Carolina and traveled westward this day near forty miles. The soil in several places was exceedingly rich and some elevated positions afforded pleasant prospects. On this road there are but few taverns; it is a common practice with every planter to keep entertainment—some make reasonable charges and others, like the ancient Britons, keep open houses for all strangers Col. B., at whose house I am this evening, is one of the latter number.

17th. To the Rev. Mr. C. The President's Proclamation for a general Thanksgiving had not reached this part till too late to comply on the appointed time. A large congregation was this day assembled to offer the Divine Being their tribute of praise. Being solicited to address them, I; with pleasure, performed the task. Whilst numerating the various privileges of Americans as men and Christians, tears of joy and gratitude witnessed the heartfelt satisfaction of the audience. After retiring I could not help reflecting on the necessity of some regulations in the post office department as it regards remote and obscure parts of this continent. The conveyance of letters and newspapers is a debt which the public owes to every infant settlement. It is a parental duty, for such settlers stand in the same relation to government as children do to their guardians. Every free government is supported by the knowledge of its citizens, therefore to deprive any part of the community (on account of poverty) of the means of instruction is an act of despotism.

18th. A wet morning prevented me from pursuing my journey, and as it was too long to perform in an afternoon, I tarried and enjoyed the conversation of my friends.

19th. After being accompanied by a friend about 12 miles, I felt considerable distress in traveling alone through the woods—not a person or a hut to be seen for 15 or 20 miles. At length I was glad to find a house where I could feed myself and horse, all which cost me but 3½d. Although affliction cometh not from the dust, yet man is born to trouble as the sparks fly upward. The gentleman at whose house I lodge this evening has had his bones broken by a fall off a horse. I can perfectly sympathize with him from the pain I experience at this moment from a tooth.

20th. Passed over several hills which had abundance of ore; crossed the Saluda at Golden Grove; in this neighborhood I am to wait 'till a company sufficiently strong shall have assembled to march over the mountains; happily I have an agreeable situation at Brother T's.

21st. Confined to my room endeavoring to digest a system which I hope will be of service to mankind.

22d. Being the first day of the week I was anxious to go out, but prudence kept me at home; a large company that collected in the evening insisted on my preaching; thirst after knowledge should not be greater than a desire to communicate what we know.

23d. Whilst waiting, time passes, but the anticipation of future good is often the most animating cordial—we live by faith.

24th. Went abroad in the afternoon and delivered a discourse to a small congregation; afterwards read by particular request some letters on liberty and slavery; a person present, who intended to barter land for Negroes, was convinced of its iniquity and declared that he would no longer possess a slave.

25th. To Sheriff T——; this neighborhood has many respectable characters, but being so remote from navigation, they complain of want of commerce.

26th. Sheriff T. and Major H., after being out all night, brought in this morning a kidnapper of Negroes; it is a common practice to steal slaves and carry them from one State to the other and often to the Floridas.

27th. The morning was bright and serene; made an agreeable sortie and lounged among the varied trees of the orchard; the peach displayed a brilliancy which far exceeded the plumage of courts or the pearly lustre of sceptered sovereigns; the contrast created a strong commotion in my mind; I beheld the falling flower and with pleasure examined the growing fruit. But Lo! Yonder drops the mitred crown and nought remains except a barren skull from whose foraminio issued wars, death and pestilence to plague a world.

28th. What sudden transitions from heat to cold—to-day it snows; A conference or meeting of ministers commenced yesterday afternoon and is to last three days; now I shall be engaged in the service of the sanctuary; in the evening to Judge W.; this gentleman is willing to emancipate his negroes provided they could be colonised; it is the sentiment of several with whom I have conversed on the subject; their prejudices are so great against the color that they cannot bear the thoughts of granting equal privileges to the blacks whilst living among them.

29th. A considerable concourse of people assembled in the woods; Elder T. delivered to them a very pathetic farewell discourse. Some of the ministers who were expected to speak not having come, the lot fell each day upon Jonah to preach repentance to the South Carolinians.   *   *   *   *

After having spent about two months in Georgia and South Carolina he came to Kentucky and then crossed the Ohio river to East Greenville, where he addressed the United States Army and about six or seven hundred Indians on July 4th and 5th, 1795, (see oration and altar of peace.) He left East Greenville about July 10th on his return tour and came via Kentucky and Virginia back to the Northern States. He gives a graphic description of his journey on his mare Primrose, as he called her, and preached at many places along his route, but space will not permit us to print the entire diary, hence we resume it at Chester, Pa., Aug. 27, 1795.   J. T. G.

27th. Breakfasted at Chester, 13 miles; from thence to the City of Brotherly Love. Thanks be to God for bringing me thus far through burning heat and deluging rain. The roads this day were much better and the country appeared delightful with exceeding good building. Visited Bishop White, who has lately ordained a black man as an Episcopal clergyman. It seems that even Episcopalians suppose the negroes have souls. After delivering several letters retired to Dr. Rogers for the night. Peace be under the roof.

28th, Attended prayers in the University. Happy sight to see the children of rich and poor meet together in the same hall. After prayers the pupils retired to their different rooms, attended by their tutors. Let science blossom like a rose in this seminary and every useful knowledge flourish like a bay tree within its walls till time shall be no more.

29th. Visited some friends, etc., paid for Gen W—n's epaulets, 30d. What shall I say of this day? Probably some good has been done, but too little to merit a place in the journal.

30th. Preached in the morning at the Baptist meeting house. May God water the seed. Dined with Bishop White, an agreeable companion. Heard Mr. Ustick in the afternoon. Preached his birthday sermon. 102 psalm, Cut me not off in the midst of my days. Preached again in the evening in the Baptist meeting house. May the convictions intended to be made take deep root in the hearts of saints and sinners.

31st. After dinner to Penypeck. Preached in Dr. Jone's meeting house to a small congregation in English and Welsh. Come holy spirit, heavenly dove with all thy quickening powers, etc. I am confident we stand much in need of a double portion in this place.

Sept. 1st. A day of rest, yet I begun a work which I hope Providence will smile upon and cause it to be one of the greatest blessings of my life.

2nd. Through a thickly settled and well cultivated country to Hopewell, N. J. Crossed the Delaware at Taylor's Ferry.

3rd. Through New Brunswick to Scott's Plain. The Lord have mercy on the poor travellers if they are always obliged to pay $1 for dinner.

4th. Through Elizabethtown, likely to kill my mare in bringing her to the boat. Arrived at New York late in the evening. A man should always keep the old resolution never to go by water when he can go by land.

5th. Received a whole bundle of letters from Wales, which will take me a long while to answer.

6th. Preached in Welsh in the morning, in the afternoon in English for Mr. Dunn. Heard Mr. Stoughton in the evening.

7th. Delivering letters and visiting old friends.

8th. Very wet weather. Preached in Welsh in the evening. Oh my poor countrymen, my poor countrymen. May God provide for you.

9th. Still trotting from place to place. Dined with Dr. H. Smith.

10th. Mr. and Mrs. H. Drowley, where I slept last night, were both taken ill of the reigning fever. Wrote a Welsh letter for the press. Went on board the packet for Rhode Island. No wind. Returned to town. Preached for Stanford, "Irish Liberty."

11th. Rather calm in the morning, passed through Hell Gate about 9; from noon till night a charming breeze. It is delightful to behold the prospects we had this day in the state of New York, Long Island and Connecticut. We came in sight of New Haven just before dark.

12th. In the night the wind changed and has continued right ahead the greatest part of the day. A warm combat about slavery. Came to anchor off Newport about 9; about 10 the health officer came on board; finding us all well, we were permitted to come to the wharf.

13th. Landed this morning and breakfasted at the Liberty Cap coffee house. Delivered my introductory letters. Preached in the forenoon for Mr. Patten, a Congregationalist. In the afternoon for Mr. Thurston, a Baptist. In the evening for Mr. Eddy. I had large congregations in the afternoon and evening and the people appeared all day tolerably attentive. Although I had a hind cold something constrained me this day to preach longer than usual. May God water the seed.

14th. Visited the Newport duck manufactory. The sight of it did my heart good. How I do rejoice to see industry encouraged. Here I saw a great number of the American fair employed like rope makers in spinning the hempen flax. Health and vivacity appeared on every cheek and their nimble feet whilst running for the next thread, caused an equal circulation of the blood through every member. Charming nymphs, heaven protect you from the foes of virtue and if I know of any who want industrious and handsome wives I will send them to the Newport duck manufactory.

After viewing the inside of the state house we took a walk round the town, which is pleasantly situated on a capital harbor but few miles from the sea. The prospect from the out lots of the town is very pleasant. The surges of the sea washing the rocks on one side and the mainland appearing in different directions on the other. The windmills, groves and natural rocks, like grottos, adorn the scene. Considering the situation I am surprised the town appears so shabby. Bad frame houses, worse streets, no foreign trade. This may be the cause of so little improvement.

In the afternoon we took a ride on the Island, the Sacred Island which gave birth to civil and religious liberty. The evening turned out foggy, a circumstance which very often deprives the traveler of many pleasing prospects in this part. Drank tea about 9 miles out of town, and returned very much pleased with my jant. Expounded the 66th Psalm to a company of Negroes, &c, in the evening, and now I shall retire to rest under the shadow of Jehovah's wings.

15th. In the packet to Providence; delightful scenes; left Bristol and Warren to the right, both very smart little towns; hills and dales, rivers and mountains form the romantic appearance of this country; landed at Providence about 3; called on President Maxey, Dr. Gano, Mr. Benson, &c. One should suppose by the appearance of this place that it requires but little self-denial to become a Baptist. Fine majestic college; one of the most elegant places of worship on the continent; the highest steeple or tower in America. Thus the poor despised B——ts are elevated above their neighbors in ye State of Rhode Island. They claim the first establishment of this State. Being persecuted by the Presbyterians from the east, they fixed their tents on this spot, and called it Providence. The immortal Roger Williams was at their head. This man, who was a native of Swansea, in Glamorganshire, has the honor of being the first leader of a sect who did not establish his opinion as the religion of the State. I am almost proud that this honor belongs to the despised B——pts. It is true the Quakers, in every instance but one, have followed their example—but this act of Roger Williams and his company was antecedent to the settlement of Pennsylvania by the illustrious William Penn.

16th. Visited the college, a very commodious building commanding a very extensive prospect down the river and in every direction across the country. To attempt a description of this situation would but diminish its praise. The commencement is but just over—sorry I am that I could not possibly attend. The students at present are not more than 90. Such a situation and such a president as Maxey ought to command double the number.

I shall say nothing of the library only, yet it has increased, is increasing and ought not to be diminished. The museum, although in its infancy, pleased me much. Part of the philosophical apparatus presented by one of the professors, Dr. Fobes, will do him immortal honor.

Fair seat of science, flourish far,
Beyond the reach of cruel war;
Let light effulgent still increase,
Within thy walls, to insure peace.

17th. Not very well—nay but I am very poorly; between the heat and mosquitoes I must exercise patience; a slight touch of the diarrhea—however, I preached in the Baptist vestry to about 200 people; the meeting-house would be too large—80x80 with double galleries on each side, and treble in front; it is actually the best place of worship I have ever yet seen; attended a funeral with Dr. Gano—nothing done but praying at the house; all the people as still and mute as a stone; drank tea with Senator Foster and Dr. Drowne, the latter a most modest diffident man.

18th. Left Providence; I hope Providence will not leave me, but I had strange commotions in my mind this morning; an American fair—yes, one of the fairest I ever saw, sat at my side in the coach—meekness and modest sat on her cheek; everything spoke here the virtuous maid; what heart would not be attracted to her? But, alas—she is the coachman's wife! Full-dressed with caring, snow balls, &c! Turn my eyes from beholding vanity—all the beauty in the world is but skin deep; in the evening to Boston; put up at Col. Emes.

The country we passed through this day was generally stony and broken. By mere dint of industry it has been cultivated and become thickly settled; good orchards and tolerable houses; good aftermath and tolerable cattle, in some places.

19th. Visited Dr. Stillman, who received me very kindly; ditto on Rev. Mr. Baldwin; walked up and down the town, which appears to be full of business, and has been of late full of faction on account of the British treaty.

20th. Preached in the morning for Dr. S-lan-n; a crowded audience in a meeting house 78 feet by 56 feet; very attentive, although I exceeded the bounds of the usual time in my discourse. Preached in the afternoon for Mr. Baldwin, to a very decent assembly, but not quite so large as Dr. S.'s. I am highly pleased with the conduct of the Bostonians; they seem to pay great attention to what is delivered; they appear affable and cheerful in the streets. My friend Dr. S., I find, is very much respected by all denominations and classes among them. Here the American fair excel; here I need pray let me not be led into temptation.

21st. The first day of the French year. The morning was ushered in by ringing of bells and firing of guns. I went to see the procession. French and Americans, with Dutch, French and American colors flying. The sign of the balance, and ye day the French Republic was established; may it be auspiciously commemorated to the end of time. Visited some friends with the Dr., who has as much work as he can very well do, to visit the sick, &c.

Wrote to Mrs. L., Carmarthen, and Mr. Dr. Richards, of Lynn.

22nd. Took physic; dined at Mr. Newnham's; read a few lines and acquired a little knowledge.

23rd. Visited Dr. Morse, author of the American Geography. He thought to reason with the mobility whilst burning Jay's effigy. He received a wound in the forehead, not intentionally, but accidentally. A certain man formerly told his friend, who had been abused by the mob, "I wonder they did not knock your brains out." "O," said the man "They could not do that, for if I had any brains, I would not have gone nigh them." I do not mean to apply this to Dr. Morse, for he is certainly a very sensible, judicious man, and deserves well of his country, but we happen sometimes to calculate too much on our own popularity. Spent the evening among the Bostonian fair, whose charms are sufficient to captivate the heart of an angel. (My remarks on the bridges and public edifices of Boston must be inserted in my last day's journal before I leave the place).

24th. Wrote to Mr. Ben Davies, H. West; walked up Beacon Hill, where a large monument is erected to commemorate the most striking events during the late Revolution. The prospect from this hill is beautifully diversified—the town of Boston in every direction falls under the eye; the little islands obstructing the river in its direct course to the ocean, which forms a majestic appearance at the distance of about six miles. Look to the country—the scattered villages, with their prominent spires, country seats, with their rural walks, meet the eye in every direction. But yonder is Bunker Hill, where the famous battle of June 17th, 1775, with the British was fought. There the monument of Gen. Warren and his associates, who fell on that memorable day, stands erect, to inspire the hearts of Americans to resist despotism and oppression. Dined at John M. Stillman's and spent the evening at home.

122

25th. Spent the greatest part of the day at Charleston and walking alone about Bunker's Hill, thinking of the valiant soldiers who fell there. On the monument I found the following inscription: "None but they who set a just value on the blessings of liberty are worthy to enjoy her. In vain we toiled, in vain we fought—we bled in vain; if you our offspring want valor to repel the assaults of her invaders." Dined at Dr. Morse's in company with several of the cloth; mostly violent against the Democrats and in favor of the treaty; I wanted them to consider the following definition of the words Aristocrat and Democrat as given in yesterday's paper.

Being in company a few nights ago with a number of young men, and the discourse turning upon politics and among other things, the words Aristocrat and Democrat were mentioned. One of the young men asked another what the meaning of the words were? He made answer—

A mbitious
R obber an
I mpudent
S lovenly
T urbulent
O utrageous
C rafty
R igorous
A rtful
T urk

or one who wants an arbitrary government, and a share in the administration thereof.

D ecent
E nticing
M odest
O bliging
C areful
R eligious and
A miable
T radesman

or other good citizen who wishes a government founded on the rights of the people, or one who endeavors to support such a one when established.

Spent the evening at Mr. M. Stillman's, in company with Dr. Still and Thatcher, Messrs. Balch, &c, &c. Poor Randolph is roasted. One modest clergyman from the S. W. Territory wanted to strangle him; he wanted to do the same with the western insurgents. This is a modest aristocrat who affirms that all those who oppose the treaty are the children of Belial and absolutely possessed by the devil. He prays with a vengeance that Old Nick may be cast out of them—but I am afraid if he breathes upon them the Evil Spirit will be more likely to get into them, than out of them.

26th. Took a ride in the coach after dinner to Cambridge and Fresh Pond; the latter is a place of much resort about five miles out of town. The situation must be very agreeable in summer. Such a large fresh water pool and variegated hills about it must afford agreeable sensations in the mind of a citizen involved with business. Here we drank tea at the public hotel, the only house in the place.

At Cambridge we went to see Harvard's College the largest, saith Morse, in the Union. The library contains about 12,900 volumes, which are well arranged. The museum contains several Indian curiosities worth seeing. There are generally from 120 to 150 students instructed at this place. The Congregationalist have not shown great liberality in taking the sole management of this college to their own hands, since Mr. Hollys, a Baptist from London, was one of the first and principal patrons of the institution.

27th. I never dreaded going to the pulpit so much as this morning; a violent diarrhea kept me going the greater part of the night, and even till meeting time—I ventured, however, and through mercy found no ill consequences; preached in the morning at Dr. Stillman's, in the afternoon for Mr. Baldwin. "As thy day is so shall thy strength be." Blessed promise! let me die whenever my strength to do good fails me.

28th. Very poorly; heavy and spiritless; did little more then lying down this day; saw a wedding in the evening at Dr. S.'s; a black couple genteely dressed in silk and satin, &c.; these are the blessed effects of liberty; God grant the French may never lay down their arms until the whole human race are emancipated. But I am told the free Negroes do not behave as well as they ought to do. Is it any wonder? Let us consider the inequality of their education and the general prejudices which prevails among the Whites in America against them. Still they are obliged to acknowledge that as they increase in knowledge they become better citizens. I do not wish to exalt the Blacks above the Whites, but certainly they claim an equality of rights.

29th. The Boston papers do little more at present than abuse each other, and of course abuse the public who are obliged to read their trash. Jacobites Jacobins, Aristocrat, Democrat, Federalist anti-dito, and worse than all personal abuse on both sides of the question, and men, who have and do deserve well of their country, but perhaps are too old to act with much energy on such occasions as the present. But my question is: "When shall ye time come?" "When the sighs of the slaves shall no longer expire in the air of freedom!" Ye seekers of power; ye boasters of wealth; ye are the Levite and the Pharisee who restrain the hand of charity from the indigent, and turn with indignation from the weary worn son of misery. But sensibility is the good Samaritan, who taketh him by the hand and consoleth him, and poureth wine and oil into his wounds."

30th. Visited the lard manufactory, which is supposed to be superior to any in Europe. I was happy to see the whole process. Happy am I always in seeing the noble inventions of man as well as the superior works of God. It is probable we only begin to know the powers of mechanism; for as we carefully turn over the leaves and examine the contents in the book of nature many mysteries unfold themselves to our view which will still add new discoveries in the book of arts.

Preached in the evening at Dr. S.'s. It is enough to inspire a dead man to preach to see 1400 attentive hearers of a week-day evening, and withal to hear the sweet singers of Israel warbling their melodious voices to the skies. O, I am in raptures of love with this assembly, which has sans doubt, the best choir of singers I have heard on this continent.

Peace and prosperity attend the whole family of Stillmans to the end of time. I am sorry my debt of gratitude cannot be extended to many more of the Bostonians. They are polite, and will ask you to come and see them, but I am an insignificant Welshman. Adieu.

Oct. 1st. The exertions of last night increased my complaint; I was obliged to take an emetic this morning; imprudently went out to dinner, which brought on a fever in the evening. If self-preservation is the first law of nature, I am often guilty of transgressing the first commandment. I am afraid I shall have much to answer for imprudencies of conduct in regard to my health.

Oct. 2nd. Something better. However, I kept my house all day; spent the greatest part of it in reading Backus's History of the Baptists in New England. Strange that men fleeing from persecution should be guilty of the most horrid persecution themselves. Peace be with the ashes of Roger Williams, who first established liberty and equality at Providence. I wish, if possible, to obtain a history of this great man's life, that the public may see the character of the first founder of liberty in America.

3d. Heard Dr. S. in the morning; preached in the afternoon; attended the conference in the evening. It appears as if the Almighty for some wise purposes meant to afflict me every Sunday morning. This morning I was obliged to return to bed, yet in the afternoon I found strength beyond expectation to preach—the Lord's name be praised.

4th. Spent the day principally at Dr. S.'s; determined to beat another retreat, which is the 2d since last July; the first occasioned by the British, the 2d by illness, being too poorly to undertake a journey alone, besides other avocations calling me back to Pennsylvania.

5th. Wrote to R. Furman, Charleston, and E. Hills, Savannah; started at 3 o'clock in the stage for Providence; dissipated company. It appears to me yet the inhabitants of this country are running a race as it were against time in the road to every manner of corruption. As for boarding houses, taverns, etc., they are in the way to cure some of their mania, for they never scruple to charge as much again as they ought for almost every article; travelled 'till after ten; supped and paid nine pence for lying down only three hours—sleeping was out of the question with me.

6th. Arrived at Providence by 6 o'clock; after breakfast laid down a few hours, and attended the examination of some fresh students at college. After dinner heard two of ye highest classes repeating some pieces on the stage. I was highly gratified in hearing some of them pronouncing with so much energy. Visited some friends in the evening, viz., Mr. Brn., Mr. Fr. and Mr. Bu. Retired to the college house; here let me rest under the shadows of Jehovah's wings.

7th. How have I spent the day? What have I done, besides reading Washington's letters? A most astonishing character to be sure. He must have a world of patience. Cool and deliberate in all his actions, he gained the esteem and confidence both of Congress and the people. Determined in his plans, he could not easily brook disappointments. However, he was taught by a train of misfortunes to give way to ye contingencies of the times, and never wanted courage to renew the action whenever an opportunity offered.

8th. By some strange infatuation I am kept half idle—a life I hate. Visited a few friends, if I can call them so. The New Englanders, of all men I have ever seen, are the worst untowardly towards strangers. There are a few exceptions, undoubtedly, but upon the whole I wish myself in Pennsylvania.

9th. Impute not sin to thy servant, O Lord. Chastise me not in thy hot displeasure. Remember I am dust, and strengthen my frame; let me go forth in Thy name and declare Thy glory to the heathen. Spent the greatest part of the day on my bed, faint and feeble.

10th. A very wet, stormy day; heard Mr. Gano in the morning preaching to a few men in his large meeting house. I never saw such an opportunity before; only one woman ; poor delicate ladies. I preached in the afternoon to about four times the number we had in the morning, the weather being something better. Ah! fine weather professors, do you expect the sun to shine upon you all ye way to Heaven? (The above statement is a day behind).

12th. Left Rhode Island State ; entered Connecticut by Plainfield, to Norwich ; slow traveling ; bad country. The hand of industry alone can make it tolerable. Norwich is upon the whole a pleasant situation and contains a great number of houses scattered about. Put up at Brown's, a good inn. Distance from Providence, 45 miles.

Last 12th of October I landed in America. I commemorate the day with songs of thanksgiving for my happy deliverance from the house of bondage and the yoke of despots.

13th. To New London (14 miles), after waiting one hour for breakfast. Set off for Saybrook (15 miles); crossed the Connecticut River and passed through several little villages to Guilford, where we dined—22 miles. From thence to N. Haven (13 miles). The last driver excelled all the rest. The country we passed through this day is very broken and stony, but being near the sea and inhabited by active laborious people, it appears tolerable. N. L. lies in a good situation for trade, but as yet it is but a little town. The great number of sea ports on this coast will prevent each other to rise very rapidly. On several creeks as we came along they were building sloops and brigs, &c. The navigation of the Connecticut River is rather difficult up, unless a strong wind blows up the river, the tide running down rapid and hardly perceptible.

14th. New Haven—very well laid out, for a healthy town ; but last year and this I find it has been to the contrary. Yellow fever last, and the dysentery this ; death even creeps in at the window. Visited the University. The library consists mostly of old books ; the students, for the sake of obtaining modern books, have been obliged to subscribe to have distinct libraries from that of the University. They have petitioned this day for more generous support from the Assembly of the State, who, I understand, are not too liberal, for I was present when one of the Judges of the Supreme Court resigned his office for want of a sufficient maintenance for himself and family. I heard likewise the same day three of the Judges of South Carolina defending their petitions for a greater salary, otherwise they could not support their families. Their arguments were principally the advance in the price of provisions, &c., taxes and public burthens being less, &c. Here we may trace the advantages of a Republican government. The public money is not squandered— even public officers of the highest rank are obliged to petition for an increase of salary.

15. Left New Haven early in the morning ; here I was received exceeding well by Isaiah Meigs and Dr. Derby ; I had no time to call on Dr. Dwight and Dr. Edwards ; left several letters for Middleton and Hartford with I. Meigs. The case of my friends in New York lay so much on my mind that I could not rest without knowing their welfare ; no doubt many of my friends have slept ; have left families behind them ; may be in distress ; If I can relieve them—at least I must go and see them although I am strongly invited to tarry behind. In my opinion there is something omnipotent that draws me forward. I do not know yet what it is, but I shall know hereafter.

16th. Landed in town (New York) last evening, knocked at Mr. Wayland's door. Hush said the woman in the passage, lifting up her hand. What is the matter? Mr. W. is dead, out of the fever. Hush! his brother is dying in the next room. Mr. Lee is dead, R. T. and E. S., etc., and all my friends. Stop said I, it is too much. Is such a one alive? He has been sick. I was electrified and trembled like an ashe leaf. I mustered all my powers, but it was too late. I crossed over to Brooklyn, found lodgings, slept and find myself something better this day, but I am informed of many more friends gone. Gone, I shall see them no more in this world. The widow mother, the orphan weeps and shall I refrain? No! I will join the guardian angel to shed the crystal tear and apply the healing balm to the afflicted spirit wherever I meet him. Wrote to Daniel Jones, Swansea, and Daniel Davies, Merthyr.

17th. Preached at Brooklyn to a small society in the morning, in the afternoon at the English church in New York. The absence of so many friends affected me much. Heavens, it is enough! Let the angel of death hold his hand.

18th. Passed through town, crossed at Pawler's Hook and walked to Skyler's mines, 8 or 9 miles. Quite fatigued. Many of the Welsh met me and after a long conversation parted. What will become of us. O God, let the cloud move before us and lead us where the bounds of our habitation are fixed.

19th. Having sat up last night till 3 o'clock in the morning, I felt the effect of it this day. Very sick, however, I preached in the evening to the Welsh and consulted, after, what to do with the orphans. Wrote to John of Vrechfer.

20th. Walked to New York. My limbs are strangely altered. What fatigue? Preached in Welsh in the evening. Slept in town.

21st. Called on Mrs. Drowly. Poor woman. She has to lament the loss of a most excellent husband. Crossed over to Brooklyn for I do not find myself adequate to the task of remaining in town, but if there was a particular call I think I would not flinch from the post of duty. But alas what is man? This day I heard of a man who fled into the country, leaving his wife dying without a soul to assist her with so much as a drop of water. What is still more horrid, he left two young infants to live or die with her. Humanity where art thou?

22nd. Remained at Brooklyn still waiting for my horse. Wrote to my brother and to Dr. Rogers.

24th. A day lost on board the packet.

To town and back to Brooklyn hunting for the gent who brought my mare; could not meet one another till night. Surely there must be some Providence in detaining me in town this day when I ought to be on my way to Scottsplain.

25th. Whilst preaching Welsh in the morning some emigrants from South Wales came in. For their sake I see now why I was detained yesterday.

Preached in the afternoon in English for Dr. Dann; in the evening in Welsh. May God send his blessing.

26th. After leaving directions and as much money as I could spare for the emigrants I left Brooklyn and passed through Newark, where I dined, to Elizabethtown

27th. Dined at New Brunswick.

To Princeton, put up at Hamilton's tavern; too late to visit the college.

28th. Breakfasted at Trenton; an agreeable situation. The place is of no great importance considering metropolis of the state. Crossed the Delaware. Bristol a small town agreeably situated on the Delaware, about 20 miles from Philadelphia. To my friend, Dr. Jones, in the evening. Not at home. Well then I must talk with the old lady who is as plain in her address as an honest Quaker.

29th. Spent the day in moping, reading and writing. In the evening I met a few Welsh friends and expounded a chapter to them. Thus the time goes on.

30th. Wrote to Col. Edwards and Mr. Toulmin. Spent the rest of the day in reading and conversing.

NOTE.—This ends the diary, as we have it. Doubtless more was written, and may be found some time.   J. T. G.

www.ingramcontent.com/pod-product-compliance
Lightning Source LLC
Chambersburg PA
CBHW031158050726
47495CB00019B/2473